NO MAN'S LAND

By the same author

The Voyages of Cinrak The Dapper

NO MAN'S LAND
A.J. FITZWATER

**PAPER
ROAD
PRESS**

This novel is entirely a work of fiction. The names, characters and incidents portrayed in it are the work of the author's imagination. Any resemblance to actual persons, living or dead, events or localities is entirely coincidental.

Paper Road Press
www.paperroadpress.co.nz

Published by Paper Road Press 2020

Copyright © A.J. Fitzwater 2020
A.J. Fitzwater asserts the moral right to be identified as the author of this work.

Cover art by and © Laya Rose Mutton-Rogers 2020

A catalogue record for this book is available from the National Library of New Zealand Te Puna Mātauranga o Aotearoa.

ISBN 978-0-9951355-3-6

All rights reserved. Apart from any fair dealing for the purpose of private study, research, criticism or review, as permitted under the Copyright Act 1994, no part may be reproduced by any process without the permission of the publisher.

To the Girls,
The Queens,
And the ones who went unseen.

1.

A piece of night complete with tiny stars flashed amongst the sun-dappled trees. A dog, Tea decided. It must be a dog, that fast and low to the ground.

But this dog made a sound like it was chuckling and whistling at the same time.

The dog had been shadowing Tea for a good five minutes. She squinted into the roadside pines, ready to throw her heavy suitcase.

A wolfish yip. Tea froze.

No wolves in New Zealand except at the zoo. Isn't that right, Robbie? "Sure, no wolves, weird or otherwise, or bears or tigers out in the wop-wops." He hadn't sounded convincing as he'd kissed her on the cheek, boarding that train to catch the ship to sail to ... where? Somewhere far north of the equator. Somewhere he would exchange shearing clippers for a gun.

This piece of furry night wasn't a weird wolf, but the way the dog stalked her was not entirely canine. She knew this with the same certainty that used to rush through her blood in the moments before her twin brother came home from being in a fight, again, or in those quiet times when they sat on the shed roof throwing pebbles into the creek near their house on the hill in Dunedin.

Magic? Now that was silly. Besides, how could anyone believe magic existed with someone like Hitler in the world?

"You a good boy?" Tea called into the thick roadside greenery. Her voice squeaked. Annoyed, she wet her mouth. "Come on out, there's a good boy."

That's what you say to farm dogs, right, Robbie?

Nothing. No panting. Not even that strange, jaunty whistle-huff.

The rushing pressure in her temples subsided and Tea sighed. Maybe she was too hot and tired. Her new floral dress pulled too tight under the arms. She dropped her suitcase. It was heavier than it had been that morning. Another sigh as she eased her left heel out of her new leather shoe which she'd had to stuff the toe of with newspaper. Blisters. Botheration. Well, at least they'd match the hardening calluses on her hands from the clippers Robbie had taught her to handle before he left.

Gritting her teeth, she put the shoes back on and resumed her trek down the gravel road. Not the Land Service uniform she was still waiting on, but still: new dress, new shoes. It had taken a lot of clothing rations, but Mum had insisted, as well as using some of what she'd put aside for Robbie's wedding suit. To Tea, it was out of place. Even her twenty-first birthday dress had been a hand-me-down.

Her mother had insisted. "Who knows what handsome farmers you'll meet! You'll be home from that silly job and married in a jiffy!"

Robbie hadn't called joining the Land Service silly. He'd been proud of his sister when she told him she had applied to be a land girl, alongside the other women's war services.

"You're doing your duty for King and country," he'd said, supplying her with a hug that left her uncomfortable but comforted at the same time. Mum wasn't big on hugs. "It's tough work. Heavy work. But I know you can do it, what with all you did looking after Grandad. And I know he would have been proud too."

She squeezed her eyes shut, and peach light softened her lids. Grandad. Taken by something wet and phlegmy, something that *felt yellow*. The Great War had eaten him from the inside out and she was worried that this war would eat Robbie, too, now she couldn't take care of her 'baby' brother. At least when he had been out shearing, she knew he was only a day or two away. Now he was too far away for her to make a difference. He may as well have been on the moon.

She didn't even have a photo of either of them, to remember. Mum didn't like those 'soul-stealing things'.

"Toughen up, girl." Tea could hear her mother's voice in her head.

Grandad hadn't been tough in those last days. He'd lost the ability, or maybe the will, to talk, the only sound coming out of him that awful, rattling cough.

"I'll punch Rommel for you," was the last thing Robbie had said as he boarded the train, laughing at her downcast face. Mum had expressed her disapproval of punching and pouting; it was *especially* bad behaviour. Such an admonishment sounded ridiculous considering the arms Robbie would be taking up.

Stop. None of that. She wasn't a child anymore. She had her war duty to do, like any good girl. All of her fantasies about the world holding a secret in store for her came from those silly books Grandad had shared with her. Elves, mermaids, dragons, monsters, fairies and queens. There were no such things. It was time to grow up. She had to know her place.

But with the men gone, the call for the women to do their part, her place had been turned topsy-turvey. Every step down this road was a step towards the unknown. Tea had a job to do, if she could only find the MacGregor property. And get away from the strange dog.

She blew her frizzed front curl out of her eyes. The latest fashion for painstakingly manicured rolls would never survive the North Otago heat. She giggled at the thought of Betty Grable wrangling sheep as she paused again and extricated from her purse the envelope embossed with the Women's War Service Auxiliary seal.

The address in the letter gave her no clue as to how far she still had to go. If she weren't careful, she might get completely lost, walk all the way up the Pigroot, and end up in the middle of Central Otago nowhere. The Palmerston concept of 'road' differed greatly from that of Dunedin. "Up thataway," the station master had nodded when no-one had been at the train to meet her. "Five miles or so. Not far."

Her blistered heels protested that 'not far'. Now she wished she had stopped at the tea rooms for a cuppa.

She hadn't seen any vehicles since she'd left the main road, the valley steadily growing narrower and steeper alongside the Shag River, but that wasn't unusual considering petrol rationing had been in place for almost a year. Only sheep and cows stared or scattered at her approach.

Oh, and there was the shadow and chuckle of the dog again. The shadow wriggled as if a heat shimmer rose from the road, a shimmer echoed in the strange squiggle that settled in her belly.

"Bother and damnation," she said.

Enjoying the sound of her blasphemy, she said it again, louder, though her heart sped. Would someone leap out of the trees and slap her for her impudence? Or would her canine shadow take it upon itself to bite her?

The whistle-huff again, like the dog was laughing directly at her thoughts. Tea stared into the trees, tried her own whistle – a terrible, slobbery thing – but the dog didn't appear. With a sigh and a wiggle of her shoulders against the unladylike sweat dripping down her back, she read her letter once more in an attempt to soothe herself.

The seal should have been that of the Women's Land Service, but the office said they were still in the process of changing to the official name. No matter how much she'd squeezed her eyes tight and wished, it didn't turn into the seal of the Women's Auxiliary Air Force, Women's Auxiliary Army Corps or Women's Royal Navy Service.

She'd volunteered early for the Women's War Service Auxiliary, hoping to be manpowered to somewhere fancy like Wigram or Ohakea. Even the WAAF station at Taieri would have been great, if a little close to home. But, tempted by a rousing speech from MP Mary Grigg to a little-attended afternoon tea at church, and Robbie's love for the countryside, she had forwarded her name to the Land Service. How strange it had been when the recruiter focused on her posture, dress, and quality of her shoes! How on earth would any of those help on a farm? Surely her nimble gardening fingers and heavy-lifting ability from nursing Grandad were more important.

She'd felt conspicuous on the train with her lack of uniform or even a badge – the Service alluded they would be forthcoming *if* she survived one month on the job. All she had were ugly gumboots and overalls to denote her call to duty, and she didn't want to show them off to the other girls in their trim blue uniforms and smart hats.

"Oi! Gittin beyind, ya filthy mongrel!"

Tea flinched, and her purse shut on her finger. She yelped. Who would use such filthy words as a greeting to a girl? "Hello?"

"Who's that?" A figure pushed through the tall, fluffy toetoe, weapon propped casually on one shoulder, prancing dogs at his heels.

Tea gulped down the taste of her heart. It wasn't a weapon, just a spade.

"My name is Dorothy Gray. I'm looking for the MacGregor farm. Can you help me please?"

The heavy rhythmic thunk of hooves. A horse too big for the pallid boy atop pushed through the tussock and picked its way onto the gravel road. She bit her lip, annoyed at her surprise. *This isn't Dunedin anymore, Tea. You must pay attention to the smells, like Robbie taught you.*

Dogs rushed her legs, but they danced rather than nipped. They *were* good dogs. And they *were* dogs, she was sure of *that* smell. The other dog, the strange one in the bushes, had smelled different.

How silly, she admonished herself.

The older man, dressed in sagging dusty pants and a red bush shirt, stepped to the fence line. His spade clanged against the wire; 'number 8', Robbie had called the ubiquitous fencing material.

"I'm MacGregor." He sized her up too slowly for her liking. "Gray, huh? I know a shearer named Robbie Gray. You his thing?"

Tea set her shoulders like Robbie had taught her too. "I'm his sister. I've been sent here from the Land Service."

"Huh. That's right. Was expecting you on the evening train. Hmm. Robbie said something about a sister once. Didn't expect a girl to follow in his footsteps." MacGregor eyeballed Tea in a way that made her scalp prickle despite the warm spring afternoon. "You're awfully dark for Robbie's kin. You not one of them lazy mowrees, are ya?"

Tea didn't hesitate; Mum hated such inferences, too. "No, sir. I simply take the sun easier than he does. We're twins."

"Huh." MacGregor looked unconvinced. "Gonna have to put that hair of yours up. None of those pins and rollers round this place."

"I understand, sir."

"You better have your gear, girl." MacGregor lifted his chin at her attire. "Them gloves are useless out here and Mrs MacGregor don't have time to be wasting on mending and frilly sewing."

"Yes, sir. These are my Sunday clothes, sir." She hefted her suitcase. "I have overalls and such, from the Land Service."

"Fine, fine." MacGregor waved her words away like a fly. "A boy and girl twin, you say? You don't got Robbie's hair or much of his face."

"Fraternal twins, sir," chipped in the skinny boy on the horse. He too had been watching Tea too close for her liking. The shivery rush of blood made her vision tunnel and she had to take a deep breath. "Means they don't always look the same. Like Robbie can have brown hair and Miss Gray can have black."

MacGregor grunted and kicked at one of the dogs snuffling near his shoes. It yipped and slunk away with a baleful backward glance. Shame pinched at Tea's throat.

The boy bent forward a little and tipped his floppy brim hat, showing off big ears and a peeling, beaky nose. She was glad he couldn't offer a hand from that height; he might crumble at a stiff shake. Or a breeze. "Nice to meet you, ma'am. Robbie told me a lot about you. I'm Grant Stevenson."

The prickle went through her scalp again. *And Robbie didn't tell me anything about you at all*, Tea thought.

"Call me Tea. Everyone does."

"In my farmyard, you're Miss Gray, girl," MacGregor snapped. "Grant, give her your seat and take her up to Mrs MacGregor to show her the ladies' cottage. Don't be late for dinner."

"Yessir." Grant tipped his hat again.

"There you are, you little bitch!" MacGregor bellowed, heaving a dirt sod at a slinking dog. Tea jumped and set her molars. "Gittaway now!"

A border collie, mostly black with a scattering of white on the bib and paws, yelped and skittered. Her shadow! It wasn't male after all. The look the dog cast back at Tea made her shiver for a third time. The familiar-strange scent hit Tea, making her flinch. It was a scent she thought she'd only dreamed, one she associated with starlight, fresh turned soil, warm cotton.

The night-and-star dog tore off, folding and stretching to avoid snapping teeth and pejoratives. The trees swallowed the farmer up, the yipping of dogs a trailing cloak of noise as they crashed through the flax.

"The driveway is a few hundred yards up that way, beyond the macrocarpa," Grant pointed. He bent forward as if to slide off the animal.

"It's alright. I've walked this far. I can walk a little more."

"At least let me take your suitcase."

"Alright then."

Her heavy heels joined the slow clop of the horse's hooves.

There was something long about the boy's face. Sharp, stubborn, but not conniving – like Robbie after one of those nights out dancing, but he had never looked quite this ill.

Closer, she could see he wasn't quite a kid after all. There were deep lines around his mouth, and though his hairline was already receding it was a pretty, silvery blond. The knuckles of his long fingers were too large, like Grandad's had been. She guessed Grant might actually be slightly older than her. A sickly one then, still working on a farm, and not conscripted.

"Sorry there was no-one there to pick you up in town," Grant said, letting the reins drape. The horse swayed along at a pace that was considerate of Tea's blisters. "We thought you were coming in on the evening train, not the express to Christchurch. We only send the carriage down to pick up empty milk cans off the evening train on mail and shopping day. Besides, the girls were fixing the shearing shed roof today. The Dodge is parked up on blocks because of petrol rationing. We only take the truck out when delivering a load of wool."

"I understand. What was the name of that dog Mr MacGregor yelled at?"

"Which one?" Grant straightened – Tea could almost hear his knobby spine creak – and tipped his hat back.

"The black border collie with the white patch bib."

"They're nearly all border collies, ma'am. Mr MacGregor breeds them."

"Please call me Tea."

"Yes, ma'am."

"It was cleaner, with very dark, long fur. And it had a speckled bib, like …" She didn't want to say it, to give him that poetry, but he was watching her with what seemed such an open smile. "Stars in the night sky."

Grant shook a fly off his face. "I don't know the one you mean."

She sighed. He had that sour lie smell about him she recognised now her senses were realigning to the country, but she had to let it be. Maybe he was another one who didn't like her taking a man's job, though he was being friendly enough as a front.

They turned into a cut in the trees. A field dotted with horses swept up to a large wooden farmhouse, painted white, with leadlight windows like large eyes. Smoke curled from the chimney even on a warm day such as this. Barns topped a rolling ridge carpeted with spring splendour. Cottages – sleeping whares, Grant called them – peeped through the pines. She vowed to enjoy the green as much as possible; already, patches were turning brown in the hard Otago sunshine.

A figure stepped out and claimed the veranda like the Queen

consort of the farm. She watched their progress, arms folded across her chest. Mrs MacGregor. Tea shaded her eyes against the mid-afternoon glare to get a better look at the staunch, solid figure, and shivered. For a moment, the silhouette could almost be her own mother's. She'd only just left, and this was supposed to be a new beginning. What ridiculous rules would she have to endure under this new matriarch?

And where did that strange dog go?

2.

Izzy smelled the new girl before she saw her. As she came up the path to the worker's cottage, slapping dust out of her overalls and cramp out of her thighs, a scent tickled her face, redolent of fermenting rēwena bread crossed with the warmth of skin fresh out of cool water.

She paused on the path just out of sight of the ramshackle girls' cottage and grabbed at shadows, weaving to her the parallel lines thrown by the tall pines along the path. Then she shook her head. *Auē, pull yourself together, girl.*

There had been someone out on the road. She'd been careless, earlier, got too close to the stranger. Only the excitement of the farm dogs at someone new in the territory had shaken her out of her stupidity. They'd called out to her, whipping up the scent.

And now, here the stranger was, already put to work with the others painting the cottage windows. The new girl's smell twined beautifully with the myriad scents of the farm, like she'd always been there; something on the verge of danger.

Izzy glanced back but, like a gentleman, Grant never ventured near the girls' cottage. What did he know about the new girl? The letter from the Land Service had been typically vague, and Mr MacGregor even less forthcoming.

The figure atop a small ladder stretched up, slathering the windowpanes with black paint. The bubbly glass would make it hard work to get a finish without gaps.

Frizzy black curls scrambled from the edges of the girl's headscarf, tumbling over the lacy collar of a ridiculous yellow floral blouse set against the stiff, too-clean lines of new overalls. The absurdity of the view pulled a giggle from her.

At the sound of her laughter, the girl started and peered into the tunnel of trees. "Who's there?"

"What in God's good name are you wearing?" Izzy chuckled, revealing herself. She dumped her saddle bags on the veranda and scratched at the sweat in her hair.

The girl frowned. "Hello, pleased to meet you," she said, paintbrush poised over the can dangling from her other hand. Very level. Very careful. Balanced. "My name is Dorothy Gray. You can call me Tea."

Izzy blinked, time doing that funny thing where it slowed to a crawl as her senses expanded. The girl's face! The scent made sense now. She was Robbie's sister. Robbie, te māhunga wai, hadn't said anything about her having signed up for the Land Service. Boys!

Time went on its merry way again. "Unfortunately, when I came to unpack I discovered my mother had, unbeknownst to me, repacked my suitcase with what she thought would be more appropriate work attire." Tea glanced down at her blouse as if to shield herself from the directness of Izzy's gaze. She frowned at the few black paint flecks that had already marred its sunshine state. "Apparently gumboots and my brother's hand-me-down work shirts are not the done thing to meet charming young farmers in."

Tea's tone sliced up another chunk of amusement from Izzy.

"Oh dear. At least the rest of your gear from the Land Service will be arriving soon."

"Really? More gear? I hope I have enough rations for it."

Izzy scrunched her nose up, her dark eyes crinkling at the edges. "You should be getting a hat, sou'wester, wet weather gear, more shirts. That sort of thing. Doesn't come all at once because supply lines are all over the place. And you don't need to spend clothing rations. It's supplied by the government."

What was the Service telling these girls before they sent them out into the back of beyond?

Tea shook her head, bemused. "Well, if you say so. I'll write back to Mum quick smart as well, to tell her to put the rest of my other gear on the train. That is, unless there's a telephone?"

"Mr MacGregor doesn't let the girls use the party line unless it's an emergency. And you'll also have to oil those boots up to help break them in if you don't want blisters."

"Too late." Tea angled her mouth askew.

"Oh, by the way, I'm Izzy. Short for Isabel. Larson. Isabel Larson. Yes. That's me. One of the other three land girls here." A blush? *Hold it together, girl.* She pointed along the edge of the pane. "And make sure you get into the corners. Mr MacGregor is very particular about blacking out."

Tea gestured a greeting with the brush and can. "Nice to meet you, Izzy. And thank you. I don't know why the windows need to be blacked out here. We're, what? Ten miles from the coast?"

"More like twelve."

"What would the Japs want with us anyway? There's only sheep and rocks out here!"

With a final flourish of paint, Tea climbed down, cricked her back and groaned. Izzy now found herself looking down at the girl. *No, not a girl. Robbie isn't that much younger than me, which means …*

"Mr MacGregor belongs to the Home Guard, and he takes his duties very seriously." Izzy ambled into the whare and the cool of her tiny bedroom, stripping off her dirt and sweat-streaked shirt, careful not to drop the dirty clothes on the neat, if threadbare, pink candlewick bedspread. Tea had started to follow but immediately backed out, averting her eyes. Izzy grinned into the coolness of a fresh shirt. "We're always prepared for anything, snow, storm, or invasion."

The bread and freshwater smell lingered overtop the stringent cut of paint. The new girl said nothing.

"So, you're Robbie's twin sister, huh?" Izzy called out. "You do look like him."

Tea's shadow appeared in the narrow hallway. "You're the first to say that. He's bigger in the shoulders than me."

"Who's older?" Slipping by, Izzy took a gulp from the water pitcher in the small front room. The girls used the room as a shared living space and had furnished it with tatty armchairs, a bookshelf, and a small fireplace, making the whole cottage a little cosier than its previous incarnation as the shearers' quarters. Had the new girl brought any books with her? Izzy's mind itched for something new.

"He's never said?" Tea's laughter bubbled up, sweeter than

Robbie's, but just as rich and warm. *Finally.* "I am. And he doesn't let me live it down."

Izzy paused, pretending to fidget with the matches and kindling in the fireplace. Tea cut a darker hole in the shadows of the dim cottage, like there was more than one of her standing in the same place. Izzy blinked and squinted; the doubled form resolved into one. How could this be? It didn't run in families.

Izzy blinked again and could see the warmth boiling within Tea's silhouette, something different again to the double vision. Another coldness gripped her guts. *Oh yes, it's there alright. Maybe brother and sister are cut of the same cloth.* Izzy had heard myths passed down and down again about twins.

Best to wait, watch, be careful. So very careful. People had their rules, their lines. They liked to gossip. There was a weight to darkness in this land.

A muddy collie tumbled through the front door with a clatter of claws, tongue a-flop with happiness to see Izzy.

Tea pushed it away, horrified as it stuck its nose in her crotch. "They're all over the place!"

"They like you." Izzy stepped onto the veranda, whistling for the dog.

"I just got here. They barely know me. Hey, where are you going?"

"It's time for—" The pump of the bell echoed across from the farmhouse. "—dinner."

Wiping her hands on her thighs, Tea snatched up her painting tools from the veranda and, juggling the ladder, scurried to catch up. "But how did you—"

"The dogs know."

*

Tea had smelled the question before it drew breath. It radiated as much sunshine as her blouse.

What was she wearing, the girl had asked. The wrong clothes, the wrong skin. A skin that pretended she could be a good farmhand. A skin obviously too much like her brother's – she hadn't decided if that was a good or bad thing. This was her one chance to draw a new skin over herself. Who knew how long the war would last, before she'd have to stop pretending and find a husband?

Tea blushed as she hurried to catch up with Izzy. There was another scent, mingling with the new, large scents all around. They were nowhere near as terrible as she thought she'd find them. The farm made a great blanket of awareness quite unlike her disjointed understanding of the city. She'd always been carefully attuned. Scents were warnings, heralds, rewards. She had never told anyone about this strange, heightened awareness, not even her brother. It made her sound quite mad.

She'd scolded herself for the less-than-ladylike greeting she'd attended upon the other land girl. Hunger, the strange dog on the road, and the long day had caused her peevish tone. Mum would be so cross with her if she'd heard.

But Izzy Larson wasn't Mum. Chattering far too easily about shearing timetables and mealtimes and rising at ridiculous o'clock, the person walking beside her exuded Tough.

Mum had warned her about tough girls. They wore pants, cut their hair shorter than was proper, smoked cigarettes and had loud voices, big rough hands, and too-brown skin from working outside.

But there was something comforting about Izzy's deep laugh, the still-perfect dark curls at her forehead and ears. She was big and dark as a storm, flashing diamond rain. And that scent like dog and cool night air. Terribly poetic in non-poetic times. Mum would say she'd been reading those awful books again.

"You got a sunhat in that rig of yours?" Izzy was asking as they rounded the low hill studded with native trees. On the far side of the farmyard, the dogs were snout-down in their bowls. Another girl ladled out bones and bloody chunks. The dog that had fetched Izzy dove into the mix.

"Yes, that survived the purge, at least," Tea sighed.

"Good. It's easy to get sunburn out here when you're not used to it." Izzy went on about all sorts of strange things about eating and drinking that didn't make sense.

Tea snuck another glance at Izzy's long jaw and nose. She was lucky. The width gave away nothing, while her own sometimes warranted a second look. MacGregor wouldn't have asked the same disquieting question of Izzy that Tea had been on the pointed end of earlier.

Mrs MacGregor pumped the dinner bell a second time, and Tea hurried to store away her tools.

"Bell only goes twice," Izzy explained, slipping off her mucky boots, lining them up neat, and padding into a washroom lined with a rack of oilskins, buckets and mops, a heavy kettle and wringer, and shelves with soap boxes and scrubbing brushes. Tea obediently followed suit. "Five minutes to wash up, and if you're not done in that time you go hungry."

The girl who had been feeding the dogs, all red pigtails and freckles, burst into the washroom and grabbed up the Sunlight soap. She reeked of dog. "Tuesday!"

"Sorry?" Tea paused in lathering her hands.

Izzy indicated between them with soapy hands. "Alison Twidle, Tea Gray."

Tea murmured a greeting, then, "What do you mean, Tuesday?"

"Lamb chop day!" Alison grinned.

Saliva sprang into Tea's mouth. Real farm lamb chops? Rationed lamb had been on the small side, fatless, infrequent. They did this *every* Tuesday?

Lost in her meaty daydreaming, Tea only gave half her attention to Alison's questions which were, yet again, about her brother.

They passed through the spacious kitchen where an enormous wood-run Shacklock blasted heat, and Mrs MacGregor's head twitched when she heard Robbie's name. "Later, Miss Twidle. So the poor girl doesn't have to repeat herself five times over. Here we go, ladies. Steady as you go, all the way through to the dining room, please." She handed out piled-high plates.

Tea's eyes widened at the weight of the pretty china plate. The meaty aroma of the chops mixed with the polished wood of the echoing farmhouse and charred wood from the wet-back stove.

The huge dining room featured creamy sconces, burgundy carpets, and an enormous porcelain-infested sideboard. Even the black paint on the bay window had been applied neat and smooth, adding a cool, dim glaze to the room. Izzy nodded towards a chair midway down the long table. Plates clattered. Tea almost sat with relief for her aching back but snatched her hands away from the high-backed chair when she saw Izzy, Alison,

Grant, and the other land girl waiting silently, eyes ardent on their food.

A grandfather clock in the hall ticked slow and heavy, matching the low rumbles in Tea's stomach. Everyone remained silent, not even introducing the other girl. What was her name? Mrs MacGregor had said it during the avalanche of information she'd imparted about cottage rules and mealtimes and not bringing boys to the cottage or sneaking out. Was it Karen? Charlotte?

Tea jumped when a sonorous bong from the clock welcomed Mr MacGregor into the dining room. Mrs MacGregor followed with two plates, flicking a light switch with her elbow. A chandelier denuded of all but four of its bulbs illuminated the table.

Mr MacGregor measured the gathered workers with stormy grey eyes under the dark clouds of his enormous eyebrows.

"Sit."

Chairs scraped. Izzy to her left, Grant to her right.

"Bless us, O Lord, and these gifts, for what we are about to receive …"

Tea fumbled for the words as the others mumbled along. Mum had always said grace, when Robbie wasn't around.

"… and may you safely bring our boys back home," said Mrs MacGregor at the end when Mr MacGregor paused.

Tea glanced up through her lashes. Mrs MacGregor's grey-streaked, bowed head didn't tremble. 'Our' boys? Tea hadn't seen any photographs, but then the living room and guest rooms had been deemed out of bounds. Did she mean Robbie and the other local farm lads? All of the Kiwi boys in the theatre of war?

"Amen," Mr MacGregor stated emphatically.

"Amen," mumbled the diners.

With a clatter of silverware, dinner turned into something altogether different, as everyone tried to slough off the morbidity. Tea quickly hacked off a slice of lamb and bit down. Her eyes oozed closed in delight. Two chops – *two!* – the best she had tasted in two and a half years. Real butter melted on the mound of mashed potatoes and the fistful of vibrant green beans. Thick gravy neatly adorned the chops, but Tea swirled it through everything. Made with real drippings, crunchy and dark!

"So, you're Robbie's sister," the unfamiliar girl stated.

Tea repressed a small sigh. *Robbie's sister, Robbie's sister, it's always just Robbie's sister.* She stuffed the thought down with a mouthful of potatoes and nodded.

Izzy saved her. "This is Tea," she said, somehow able to chew and talk at the same time without earning a glare from Mr MacGregor.

"I'm Carmel Atkinson." She flicked back toffee-blonde curls. "Sorry I wasn't here to meet you. Me and Izzy, we were bringing the sheep down for the next shearing."

Tea nodded back, mouth still too full. Shearing already! Were there enough boys for a gang in the district?

Thankfully, Carmel didn't ask for information about Robbie. The conversation turned towards what consumed every Kiwi's waking moment, and often their sleeping moments too. Mr MacGregor gave a report of the previous evening's news from the BBC World Service, censored for the girls' sensitive ears. He listened to the wireless religiously after dinner over his cup of tea and newspapers, Izzy whispered to Tea out the corner of her mouth.

Mrs MacGregor tempered a rousing Churchill speech and the Allies' press into Libya (*Where is that?* Tea wondered. *Must get out my atlas*), with news of a local family who had received a telegram a few days previous.

Then there was Grant in his too-big clothes, watching the conversation flow by. He chewed over every word like he chewed on his chops. Slow and careful.

Especially the ones about Robbie. The buttery potatoes loosened Tea's grip on her annoyance. She couldn't help the pinch of pride at having everyone's undivided attention. Yes, Robbie had joined the Second Expeditionary Force out of Linton. No, he wasn't allowed to say where and when he'd been deployed (she couldn't stop her stutter; did the walls all the way out here have ears?). Yes, he was still alive as far as she knew. No, she hadn't received a letter in a few weeks. Yes, she would read them later to everyone if they so wished.

They did. Grant said nothing, but when she glanced at him out of the corner of her eye as pudding was delivered to the table, there was a strange glint in his eyes. He must be jealous because he was not of a health or size to sign up.

The scent of apples, boysenberries, and brown sugar made Tea's tongue tingle. She'd emptied her dinner plate clean and her belly was tight, but by golly she was going to make room! Mrs MacGregor spooned out bowlfuls of fruit crumble with big dollops of cream. Real cream!

Somewhen back in Dunedin, her mother laughed and pinched her hip. "Rationing will be a wonderful way to help you drop that weight you've put on since you turned eighteen. No man likes a fat wife!"

Yes, it had done that. And it had also left her tired. A different tired to that of the few short years she'd spent nursing Grandad, with all that lifting to the bedroom and the outhouse. And with Robbie gone God knows where, it had left her too empty to be thinking about catching a husband.

Tea glanced right as the second-best china cups came out for the tea. Grant nodded along to something Mr MacGregor was saying about top dressing with the collected manure – *what on earth is that?* – but under the tablecloth he massaged the large red knuckles of his skinny right hand. Only then did she catch his scent. Warm clay dust and wool, rather pleasant. Why hadn't she caught it earlier?

As she started thinking up words to describe him to Mum in her letters, he gave the tiniest of grimaces. As if he'd heard her thoughts.

A sting. Tea's right hand went into a spasm, fingernails biting into her palm. Her teaspoon of sugar clattered into the saucer and black liquid sloshed on the tablecloth. Mrs MacGregor clucked her dismay. Mr MacGregor growled a warning.

All apologies and dabbing napkins, Tea flapped her hands, thinking she'd caught a splash from the pot or a wasp had made its way to the dinner table, but it was neither. A ghost sting. Her fingers were still prickling by the time the mess was cleaned up. Face hot beneath the stares from the diners, she resumed drinking her tea, wringing her fingers under the table between mouthfuls.

Grant took the tiny uproar in his stride, neither scolding nor laughing. Tea appreciated his gentle silence. Was that the tiniest of glances through his sun-lightened lashes? Tea didn't dare catch the MacGregors' disapproval a second time during the meal. It wouldn't do to be accused of anything untoward on her first day.

Her first day at *work*. Her first day away from home.

The stares whittled away as Alison and Carmel took instructions for the next day. There were groans over thistle grubbing, race cleaning, and wood chopping. Tea volunteered for the wood chopping; something she knew how to do and was good at.

Not all the stares left her alone. Izzy narrowed her eyes when she caught Tea rubbing her fingertips together. Grant too kept making a fist. Tea could hear his large knuckles creak.

*

"What happened?"

Dishes done, Izzy had been instructed to introduce Tea to all the dogs.

"When?" Leaning over the gate of the dog run, Tea let the dogs sniff her before she entered their territory. It seemed the right thing to do.

"At the dinner table. When you dropped your spoon." Izzy pushed into the dog run, inured to the nips and licks.

Wet noses pressed into Tea's hands. "A wasp startled me, that's all."

"Are you sure?"

Was Izzy calling her a liar? Tea took the road best trodden. "Well, it might not have been a wasp, but some insect crawled onto my plate …"

Izzy straightened from opening the bitches' box. She looked Tea up and down, but not in the way MacGregor had done earlier. Her age-old regard smoothed against Tea's skin like moss on stone. At the moment Izzy looked away, the sun dipped behind the sheds, and Tea shivered.

Tea's hand ached for the rest of the evening, the buzzing heat reaching her elbow despite the wriggling puddles of fur that soothed her attention. Latching on to the ones that would be her working companions was easier than she thought. They liked her scent, or so Izzy said.

Scent. For some reason, she could define each of the many dogs by their individual smells, which were not as unpleasant as she thought mucky dogs would be.

The other scent she sought from the starlight dog lingered on the breeze, but she couldn't pin it down to an individual. Was it a stray? A wild dog? A weird wolf?

Dusk had well and truly set in by the time they finished mucking out the run and scrubbing down the boxes. Even though Tea assessed the dogs' markings one by one, the pack was still one short. The night-and-stars collie that had stalked her earlier in the day was nowhere to be seen.

3.

"How much do you think she knows?"

"More to the point, I think, is how much does she feel it?"

"There's a difference?"

"It's not been that long. You don't remember?"

"It's been ten years. Might be easier for you. You were taught this stuff from the cradle."

"Yes. No. I don't know. Even if they never become like us, those who carry whaiwhaiā feel it under their skin all their life. It will be there. Depends on how strong it is, what it does to her mind."

"She's … radiating. Working warm. And I don't think she even knows it."

"Yes, I can see it. She's holding herself very tight. Too tight. She might break if she's not careful."

"She won't be the first."

"And not the first in that family, either."

"Does she know?"

"No. And it's not our place to tell her."

"She needs instruction of some kind. And soon. Or she might Split. It was a close call the last time."

"We don't know her that well. It's not going to be as easy as last time to bring it up. There were … extenuating circumstances."

"Oh, hush you. She's very close in kin to Robbie. Going untrained has its own dangers."

"Robbie got a hold of it well."

"Didn't he just."

"Is that jealousy?"

"Hush. Pass the tea. How strong do you think it is, when it runs in families? Do they share, you think? Or is it divided, like they're twins?"

"There's no such thing as sharing whaiwhaiā. It's unique to each person. I've never seen it in families, but, well, here's our first time. Its strength all depends on how much you want to accept it into your being."

"Like God."

"It's nothing like God. Don't you make that face at me."

"Don't *you* make that face at *me*. I swear—"

"Yes, I know. If I was any other girl and this was any other job. Cut it out. We're in this together."

"You know I don't mean it."

"I know. You've been fidgety lately. Your skin is raw. You really should stop rubbing it like that."

"I can't help it. There's something happening. Over there. Where Robbie is."

"Dear God. You feel those far better than me. Big?"

"Very. This whole war is a storm."

"Hey. He's going to be alright. He'll come home. I know."

"You can't know that."

"He's tough."

"And not. Come on. His skin can be too thin sometimes, when it gets too much."

"He said he was ready, that he had to do this. He practised heaps."

"And he's also an excellent liar."

"Aren't we all."

"This … this thing, between the three of us. Who is going to talk to the girl? She'll have to know, and soon, or she'll break."

"It should be up to Robbie, really."

"But he's not here. And we can't go to him."

"Guess it will have to be my job, because I'm the girl. Don't want to make it any more complicated than it has to be."

"Make it quick. Because that storm? It's coming our way. Going to overtake us all if we're not ready."

"Auē."

*

Saturday night should not feel like this.

Rocks for shoulders. Splinters of agony up her neck. A hot pain in the sway of her back unlike anything she'd endured in her lady moments. Who knew each freshly shorn sheep skin could be heavier than the last? And they kept on coming. 'Fleeco' had sounded like such a romantic title until Tea discovered the lifting, throwing, sorting. And the laughter.

Another pain settled behind her brow, the heavy memory of the sheep she'd tried to shear after the gang boys goaded her into it. Her shaking hands. Izzy's silent gaze. The boys shouting "See, girls can't shear!" MacGregor's yelling. Wasting time was as much a sin as a girl picking up shearing clippers.

Tea groaned, shoved the memory away, and tried to find a comfortable position on the lumpy mattress. Arm flung across her eyes against the glare of the single beeswax candle – was there anything on this farm they didn't make themselves? It was too early to be lying down but there was nowhere else she could put her body. Plans for the dance at the Palmerston town hall: scuppered. Distance between the water tank, the copper, and the girls' bath: too far.

She'd managed to wash her few work clothes before collapsing in exhaustion. It would be like that for a week or more until Mum could send on her more useful gear, the things she had helpfully unpacked. Thankfully her gumboots made it; she didn't have the rations to get another pair of the strictly rationed footwear. Her only useful shirt was already yellowing around the collar and armpits, and smelled like sheep no matter how well she scrubbed.

"Knock knock?" A voice of soft light.

Tea swallowed a sigh. Why expect privacy here? "Door is open."

The weight of sunshine in her doorway. "I thought you had gone to the dance."

Tea waved Izzy forward. Izzy didn't have to wait to be invited over the threshold, but she always did. "Could say the same of you. Alison and Carmel took their horses hours ago."

"Need some Tiger Balm?"

Izzy knew.

Tea swung her legs off the bed and waited for the twinkles at the corners of her vision to subside. That had been happening a lot more this week, and it wasn't usually when she was tired or upset. "No, thank you. It's too hard to come by. It's just a few aches. I'll push through."

"Don't be a goose." Izzy held out a tin reeking of menthol. "Take a scoop. I don't use it much."

Tea's hand hovered over the tin. "Are you sure?"

"Tea!" A laugh and a warning all at the same time.

"Thank you."

The emollient burned into the skin of Tea's shoulders and neck, and she let out a relieved sigh.

"Good." Izzy tossed the tin on Tea's nightstand as if it wasn't as precious as gold. "Ready for an adventure, then?"

"I beg your pardon?" Tea laughed.

"She laughs! Hallelujah!" Izzy raised her arms and danced back out the door.

That smell again! Sweet like Robbie's sweat after a night of dancing. Warm like linens fresh from the washing line. Deep as the chocolate Tea had almost forgotten the taste of.

"Have I really been such a grumble guts?" Tea asked. "Mum would be so displeased."

A thin crease appeared above Izzy's freckled nose – *like dark stars* – but it disappeared into a wicked smile. "Then it's a good thing your mum isn't here. Come on, the coals will be ready."

Tea snuffed her candle and the cottage pitched into darkness. The huge southern sky embraced the hills, stars immaculate in the moonless night. Did Robbie watch these same stars too, upside down wherever he was?

Izzy hissed at her to move quietly as they approached the farmhouse. Glenn Miller whined from the wireless in the forbidden living room.

Izzy hunched into the hydrangeas and beckoned Tea over. A tiny chink of light showed through a scratch in the black paint, so neat it had to be deliberate.

Tea froze, shaking her head. What sort of adventure was this?

"You're such a chicken," Izzy whispered, leading Tea away with a pinch of her elbow. "It's Saturday night. They'll be glued to those chairs for hours until the girls come home. It's about the only time they spend together, alone. You know Mr MacGregor sleeps in the shearer's quarters mostly."

"No?"

"It's true! They love each other, you know. Mrs M was tired of pushing out boys, and now they're all gone off to war. Why do you think there are so many land girls working here?"

"Alright, that's enough." Tea didn't mean for her low chuckle to come out awkward. Love? That didn't sound right. Love was for princesses and movie stars.

Izzy tiptoed round to the kitchen door. "It's hard enough to get placement for one land girl. The farmers don't like us much. Four on one station is nigh on a miracle."

Izzy was full of all these strange titbits about the Land Service. Sometimes it sounded like she criticised the government. Was that the treason the posters warned her too look out for? She didn't think so, but she'd been wrong many times before.

Tea slipped off her gumboots and went pad-foot across the veranda.

"Hey, what are you doing?"

"Liberating the pantry!" Izzy made it sound like some battle.

Tea planted her feet. "I am *not* stealing from the MacGregors!

That's not fair to everyone."

Silence. Whatever Izzy was doing in the pantry, she did it well. Tea hated the thought she'd had practise at stealing. More treason? Should she alert Mrs MacGregor? But that would get Izzy in trouble, maybe fired, and there was already barely enough manpower to make the farm function at proper capacity.

Tea's breath rushed back when Izzy reappeared, a basket of goodies in her hand. Izzy nodded towards the milk can in the cool room.

Saliva flooded Tea's mouth at the thought of thick and frothy cream. Before she knew what she was doing, she grabbed an enamelled cup, dipped, and dashed back out.

Izzy's grin flashed like a falling star.

With two of the quieter dogs following and Tea constantly looking back over her shoulder, Izzy humped her creaking basket of goodies over two fences and down a small hill to the creek that cut through a stand of native bush towards the river. The little stone bridge had given Tea pause each time she'd chased a bevy of forlornly shorn sheep into the holding paddock. The thought of the squirming inky bodies of eels below her feet should have disgusted her, but she often found herself bound by the hush and sway of the creek. She had missed the sound of running water without even realising it.

An impish glow beckoned from the edge of the bush. The hill and bridge did a fine job of hiding the sparks spitting skyward when Izzy nudged rocks aside with the toe of her rough work boot. A real campfire!

"Do you know how to make damper?" Izzy broke an egg into a mound of flour and gestured for the milk. Fork scraped against tin plate.

"I heard about it. Robbie said he used to make it when he was mustering up-country."

A sprinkle of raisins went into the dough, then Izzy wound the sticky mass onto two stakes, propping them over the coals. A billy of water, snuggled into the side of the fire, completed the illicit supper. Tea couldn't ignore the smells mixing with the delicious green damp from the bush. There was jam in the basket, too. The temptation from the leftover milk became too great and she took a sip. Heaven.

"You can sit down, you know." Izzy gestured to the fuzzy lumps, who were happy to act as pillows.

"What's all this anyway?" Tea said, slowly easing down. "What would Mr MacGregor say if he found out?"

"I'm on duty tonight. Sometimes when the boys have been in their cups a bit on Saturday night, they get it into their heads to rustle a sheep or two. They'd get a pretty penny in town for lamb."

The remnants of Tea's own roast dinner congealed near her heart. Would the boys try it on tonight? They were just two girls in the dark! Tea glanced at Izzy's long profile painted with the fire's red glow. No, with Izzy around an odd quietness stole into the pit of her stomach. Her shoulders softened a little. Like the times when Mum went out to play cards and she had the house to herself for a couple hours.

Dogs huffed and sighed, wetting Tea's hands with licks. The creek whispered on its never-ending journey to the sea. The stillness allowed her to poke around the memories of her first hard week. The shearing boys' laughter stung bitterly, but a cool, deep well had opened inside her, swallowed the sting, and left her with the satisfaction of a job done in messy fits, but done well.

The silence became too much. Tea grabbed at the first piece of conversation that sprung to mind.

"What is Grant's story? Why is he still here and not over there?"

Izzy turned the damper. "It's not something he's fond of talking about."

Tea ducked her head. "Oh, sorry."

"No, it's alright. He gets asked it a lot, but we're different to those nosy-pies in town." Tea couldn't read Izzy's face in the twisting light. "He had rickets as a kid. The dry summers out here in Northern Otago are good for his joints. But it stops him from being drafted."

Another sick one. The memory of Grandad coughing and twisting in his bed during the damp cold of winter rushed back at her. She'd tried to keep the fireplace stoked as high as Mum's widow pension allowed.

"What is it?" Izzy leaned forward, and the simmering coals widened her face like some demon. "You're not worried, are you? Lord, last thing we need is another girl mooning about the place. Grant can take care of himself, don't you mind."

"No, no!" Tea warded Izzy off with a spread of her hands. "I mean, Mum would think … I mean, I have to eventually … but … the war will end and … Oh, now I've torn it."

Izzy laughed and sat back. "It's alright, I'm only teasing. Grant has other things to keep his mind occupied."

"Another girl?" Her relief went to war with frustration. She hadn't really been considering him in that vein, but he'd been a suitable topic of conversation in her letters to Mum.

"Something like that. Don't be so surprised. He's tougher than he looks."

"Sorry. I mean, is it you? Would you like to court him? Once the war is over?"

"No, Tea. I don't."

The way Izzy said her name – *really* said her name, not like the way Mum barked at her – made Tea tense up. Izzy had already dismissed the conversation, bending over the fire to stir tea leaves into the steaming billy. There was something odd about her expression that the fire did not paint on, something keen and focused. Tea remembered the way girls smiled at school, the way they made friendships like war strategies, and … this was not it. Something shadowed and animal-like flickered in the angles of her cheekbones and jaw, but when Tea blinked it was gone. Must be just the fire.

The dog under her arm shifted and sighed. They danced and huffed their dewy breath each sunrise, folding and expanding at her commands. How strange to be so easily adored.

"The dogs like you." Could Izzy read minds too? "I've never seen them take so quickly to a new farmhand other than Robbie."

How did it always come back to Robbie?

Frustration warred with relief in Tea as the conversation turned to the individual personalities of the dogs, but as Tea sipped the strongest tea she'd enjoyed in many a month, she conjured up the last memory of her brother sitting on the garden shed roof, staring down the hill into the blacked-out town.

They'd shared tea then, too. He had spoken about how the Japs could fly over at any moment, but then, like now, all she wanted to hear was the hissing kek-kek-kek of a possum in the bush, a snuffling hedgehog, the whisper of the creek. His words of dances, girls, and watered-down beer had slithered like the sandstorm he was heading into. But she could read between the lines, hear the tremor of fear on his breath. He was going wherever Rommel was making his stand, a sapper going to build bridges and tunnels. That hadn't sounded right. Soldiers didn't go to *build*.

The creek ached against her senses, pulling her back to this night, this moment. Was there water where he had gone? Why did this thought tickle her so? She chewed her jam-slathered damper with eyes at half-mast as Izzy blathered on about farm animals like some schoolteacher. Underneath it all, a hiss, strong, rough-smooth. Tea's tingling skin kept her poised on the edge of leaping up and facing the hissing wall of night.

The hiss took on a scraping aspect, and she rubbed at the prickles running up and down her right arm. Water, on rocks. The creek. The eels. Eels boiling around an interloper in their territory. Eels slithering and grating, their dark, oily bodies sliding sensuously against each other, tails rubbing and flicking, barbed mouths and astonished lips gulping at the surface then arching down for more.

Tea tried to shake the waking dream away, but the slither felt so *right* against her skin, warm and wet and hungry. She'd never felt this ... no, that was a lie. In those quiet moments when the house had slept, when Grandad had found some peace for a few hours from the yellowness that ate him from the inside out, when Tea sat and watched the dying fire, she'd reached out to this scrape. More than once Robbie had found her dozing over these noises, her fingers twitching, reaching for something that wasn't there.

"Tea? Are you alright?"

Izzy. Izzy's hand on her arm. Izzy, bright as the fire, warm as the stars. Izzy's warm-sweet scent encasing her.

Izzy's face loomed too close. Tea shrieked. The parted lips, the question in Izzy's face. The darkness. Izzy caught her in a grip tighter than her fear for the gun in her brother's hands. There was the whisper – who had told her such a salacious thing? – that a look and a touch like this had killed her father. But he'd been lost to the chemical beasts of the Great War, hadn't he?

"What is it? What's wrong?" Izzy looked hurt.

"I thought I heard something," Tea said, thick and slow.

Izzy had retreated, but her hand was right there. Wrong there. On her arm. Was Izzy that weird wolf Robbie warned her about? Not a real wolf, but a predator the girls whispered about in Physical Education class at school.

And then Izzy's face changed. A smile took the whole of her eyes, making her tough angles handsome. Mum used the word to disparage a girl's ankles, but now Tea understood its true meaning. A man should be handsome, but a girl could be, too.

It had been a look of kindness. That's all. It meant nothing.

"Of course you heard something." Izzy narrowed her eyes and cocked her head, as if inspecting something deep behind Tea's eyes. "It's … the eels. They speak to you."

With that, Tea broke free of the spell. "Eels can't talk!" she laughed.

Izzy finally removed her hand, nodded, and folded her arms. "Good. I wasn't wrong about you after all. You really are Robbie's sister."

"What are you talking about?" Tea continued to laugh. She had to. The short burst of relief had been taken over by something much darker than the night. "Of course I'm Robbie's sister!"

Before Tea could turn Izzy's meaning into something real, before she failed to resist the riptide that pulled her towards the creek, another sound intruded on their camp. A thunk of hooves on grass.

One of the horses must have wandered over to investigate. The dogs looked up sleepily, unfazed by the new guest.

Big ears flicking, a long, sandy-coloured head eased out of the dark, nodding over short-stop legs.

A relieved giggle burst from Tea's lips. "I didn't know the MacGregors have a donkey." She stroked the soft petals of the donkey's nose, and like the other farm animals it didn't shy away.

"They don't." Izzy propped her chin along the L of her fingers, elbow on knee.

"A bit of a wanderer, hey? What's your name, honey?" Tea crooned.

Izzy eyed the donkey, and it bobbed its head like the silly animal was giving Izzy permission.

"Grant," Izzy said.

"You named the donkey after Grant? That's mean!"

Tea reached out for a reassuring pat, but the dirty-soft face wasn't there.

"No," said a quiet, pinched voice. "I *am* Grant."

Tea gave a little screech. The boy eased between them, reaching for the billy. Was he ... was he *naked?*

Tea leapt up. "Where did you come from? Where did the

donkey go? *Where are your clothes?*"

"Tea, sit down," Izzy ordered, refreshing a mug and holding it up.

"No! You tell me what's going on here *now* or I'm going straight to Mr MacGregor!" Tea shook as she gave the order. She'd never been so straightforward, even with her mother when she was nursing Grandad. It wasn't very ladylike. But now wasn't the time for ladylike things, other than looking away from Grant's skinny nakedness.

Izzy shrugged and passed a blanket and a tin plate of leftover damper to Grant. "Here, eat up. Changing quick must hurt."

"It does." Grant tugged the blanket around himself, flexed his red-knuckled hands, and glanced sideways up at Tea. He shoved the damper in his mouth like he hadn't eaten his fill of dinner. "Come on, Tea. Sit down. I'm not going to bite."

"I thought you went to the dance." Tea kept on her feet out of sheer perversity. Grant wouldn't hit her, no. Izzy might, if she followed through with her threat.

Grant shook his head and kept shovelling in food. Where did it all go on a body that was all bones?

Grant gave Izzy a look Tea couldn't comprehend. Something old and weary. "I thought you were going to do it," he sighed.

"Fine. Hold on."

Tea backed away a step.

An eel splashed in the creek.

With a creak like the Nor'wester through the pines, Izzy's flesh and bones folded inwards. Fur as black as her hair sprung along her spine, spreading rapidly over her hands and feet. Fingers and toes coalesced into claw-tipped paws. The star-freckles of her nose scattered into the bib and paws of the dog that had been following Tea that first day. Izzy's mouth opened wide in a toothy dog grin, and her pink tongue rolled out along with the bitter-sweet scent that had dogged Tea all week.

The scent of starlight.

Tea slapped her hands to her mouth to hold bile and scream in. "Dear God in heaven," she whispered. "You're a weird wolf!"

"Tea, we're—" The word Izzy said through her fearsome mouth was too mangled for Tea's comprehension. It frightened her. It sounded Māori.

"Like you are," Grant said, trying to sound reassuring, but Tea could only taste in her mind's eye the white skin he hid under the blanket, the *animal* he hid inside himself. "For some strange reason, the power runs in your family."

Izzy padded forward as if to greet her anew and that was it for Tea. Slipping on the crackle-dry grass, she turned and ran back towards the only other light for miles around.

4.

As the minister droned on through a prayer, Grant risked a glance down the pew. Careful had to be the natural state of things. Girls had misread these glances, and God was always watching.

Wedged between Mr MacGregor and Alison, Tea cut her stare through the edge of her eyes, the angle of her jaw taut. Grant dropped his gaze and tried to massage warmth into his knuckles. The country church exuded chill even on a sunny spring day.

Calculations danced through Grant's head. Tea hadn't dobbed them in to the boss, but she was using him as some sort of shield. He couldn't quite explain the sadness such distance infused him with. He had hoped they would be friends.

The minister swung into the sermon, making words about the sacrifice of New Zealand's good young men and how everyone had to do their piece on the home front. Grant clenched his toes. The stolid church stones mumbled to him about all the eyes that flicked over him. He was one of only a handful of men his age in the church; two of them were recuperating from injuries suffered in the line of duty, another proudly robed up in his uniform ready to depart at any moment, and the last was Mrs Mulligan's son Dwayne, a sweet man with the mind of a five-year-old.

A strange dance ensued on the ride back to the farm. Freed from the constraints of church silence, Alison and Carmel chattered about the post bag, who was and wasn't at church, next week's dance. The usually loquacious Izzy kept her peace while Tea kept her distance. Tea was still learning to handle her horse, Morgan. Grant sent soothing vibrations down through the ground in the pony's direction. Tea didn't have to know.

What did Tea see when she looked at him? A skinny boy with a cough and pale cheeks that burned too easy?

She's one of us.

Three, now four. Maybe three again. Maybe two, if … *No, don't think like that.*

Thinking of Robbie made him weave together all the times they'd ridden to and from town, even made him miss Robbie's favourite joke, how he called him a mule atop a horse.

Pull yourself together, boy.

The stones told Grant when Tea's eyes latched onto him, as if she could hear his thoughts. This wasn't just about survival; it was buried deep in his mule-ness, knowing where and when to be, where people were, what they needed. A blessing and a curse – his equine abilities lent him a strength his body wouldn't otherwise have.

Tea tugged at her gloves and fiddled with her reins, but Grant could feel her turmoil through the minute vibrations in the stones. Always the ground talking to him. He wished, endlessly, that he could tell the ground to shake something up for the boys over there, but fine control was not in his command; he was a beast of burden. It didn't stop his joints from aching, his chest tightening up when it was cold, but it was something. It was enough.

Lunchtime proved equally tense. Tea caged herself between Alison and Carmel. Meals weren't always this quiet, no matter what Tea thought of the stern mask the boss put on. Did she know about the boys the MacGregors had seen off to the front? The Missus hadn't spoken of them since they left, like she was afraid uttering their names would bring a curse down on them. A rough way to do it, but that was the Missus. Ed and Bert were good, hard-working boys, though they'd had more time for the amiable Robbie than for him.

Down the table, Izzy put on her best face. She'd better be careful. Being quiet could give her away. Mr MacGregor constantly reprimanded her for being a chatterbox, but sometimes they all needed the silence filled. Izzy had the right words. Usually. But not today.

"Right, you lot." Mr MacGregor's voice punched through the tension. "Down to the shed with you."

Carmel stacked the last of the dishes away with a mock groan, and Tea pulled on her boots silently at the back door. The shearing gang trooped from their cottage – they always ate separate – carefully pinching off the ends of their thin tobacco rollies, stomping into their boots. Dogs milled like a black and white storm. The war didn't stop for Sunday.

Sheep bleating. Izzy bellowing. The stink of male sweat mixed with hair, lanolin, and the sweet-sharp glow of the girls. Grant could separate each of the men by their scent alone. The gap in the scent palate left him fumbling with his pencil and clipboard for a moment.

A warning stitched into the air. Izzy glared at him over a bundle of freshly shorn wool she tossed onto the table for grading. He was exuding too much again. He coughed, the stuffiness of the shed making his chest tighten. Did the Missus have enough of those nice herbs dried for tea?

"You stupid girl!"

Mr MacGregor's bellow startled the shed into a portrait of frozen wonder, the gang boys leering, Carmel's face twisted in pain and surprise, a sheep all tits-up.

Then, a burst of action. Carmel's shears twanged into the floor of her run, and she shrieked. The sheep bolted for freedom. The shearing gang laughed. Alison flailed her arms in a wild attempt to block off the sheep.

The strange hot twinge flared in Grant's knuckles at the same time Tea made her move. Girl and mammal went down in a roll of legs and hooves. The sheep mah'd its discontent as she wrestled it back into the run. Her face set in stone, Tea snatched up Carmel's shears, locked right leg and left arm into the correct position and clipped away. The gang boys scoffed harder, then fell silent as Tea clipped smooth and steady.

Only the disgruntled sheep waiting in the gates made a sound.

Grant watched, fascinated, as Tea kept the ewe calm, muttering under her breath, the shears almost an extension of her hand. She'd been taught well, her technique smoother than Izzy's, who often treated the sheep like the eye dog she barely kept harnessed inside herself.

"Alright, stop gawping," Mr MacGregor grunted. He

narrowed his eyes at the gang boys, and they looked everywhere but at the boss or Tea. "Carmel, gittup to the house and see the Missus about that hand. The rest of you, gitton. These sheep don't shear themselves."

Hand wrapped in her handkerchief, Carmel sniffled and hurried away. Grant kept his silence – the gang boys placed him only just above the land girls in respect – and went back to grading the wool, picking out imperfections, notating bale weights, all the while keeping an eye on the smooth job Tea performed upon the now relaxed ewe. She had a way with the animals, that was for sure.

Within nine minutes by the shed clock the fleece fell away from the ewe in one clean piece. Faster than some of the shearing gang.

"Attagirl!" Izzy whooped, punching the air.

Ignoring the praise, Tea pulled another sheep into the run and set to. Izzy threw the fleece on the table, and Grant checked it over. Tidy edges, even clip. Izzy gave him a tiny nod. The girl had style.

After eight more sheep, Tea wasn't exactly smiling, but there was a straightness to her back that hadn't been there before. Grant watched her as she went to wash up for dinner. Her stride seemed longer, too. She'd made a decision.

Returning to the solitary of the men's cottage – *Buck up, cheerio, it's not for long* – he checked his kit once more. He wanted to be prepared in any case for what Tea's decision might be. He had to be.

How could he give this up so easy, especially on the whim of a girl? This was all he had. There was no going back south to

45

Gore. This was *home*. It was safer here; at least it had been, before the war.

*

Tea had *smelled* the way Grant looked at her all through Sunday, a far too pleasant mix of dust and hay. The air shivered with it, an aptitude all at once familiar and unfamiliar for its normality. She'd always been able to tell when Mum was opening her mouth to speak, or when Robbie was sneaking through the house, by the shift of the air. Now that she knew it was *magic*, the pull of it sat ungainly around her face, the air rough with too much possibility.

Questions squeezed her brain and chest as she tried to wash off the sheep muck in time for dinner. Carmel and Alison called back and forth, the slight injury of the earlier afternoon almost forgotten. Strangely enough, Izzy remained quiet, though her presence pressed large against the air, making Tea feel like she was gasping for breath.

"Wolf in sheep's clothing on one side, mule boy on the other," she muttered to herself, splashing water on her sweaty face and neck. "And now I think eels can talk to me? Why didn't you tell me, Robbie?"

Because there's no way you would have believed me. You have to see everything for yourself, you stubborn goat.

She paused, hands plunged in water that was still painfully cold even after being humped up from the creek. The water tried to whisper a reassurance over her skin, and she flinched. Now she was imagining her brother's voice as well as the hissing voice of this strange magic Izzy and Grant claimed she possessed.

Like them.

No. She couldn't be like them. Especially Izzy. A wolf that talked to her, looked at her like a man would a woman. Was she becoming too mannish already with all this man's work? Mum had said to be careful of that. Men wouldn't want to marry a mannish woman. No man wants another man. She'd once said this too loud in front of Grandad, and he'd got this expression that pushed so hard against the air. Tea had been so confused by the whole altercation, and ashamed too, of her blunt fingers, her desire to hold shearing clippers as competently as her brother.

The banging of the dinner bell startled Tea back into the real world, and she rushed to dry off and dress. The inadvertent soak hadn't been enough to remove the dirt settled under her fingernails.

Oh my gosh, the shearing, they let me do it! The thought tingled along her skin like cold water, buzzed around her teeth and lips, warmed her belly. It was a mark of how the work was getting under her skin.

Had it only been a week since this all started? Yes. And no. And forever.

I can't go back home now. I can't fail at this, no matter whether Izzy wants to turn me into some sort of man. Or beast. I don't know what I'll do with this magic, or them, but I'll do it for Robbie.

Good enough for the time being.

The creek hissed at her as she made her way to dinner. The sound followed her everywhere now, had *been* following her for as long as she could remember: water in the pipes; the small creek near her house; the waves in Dunedin harbour that should have been too far away to hear; her menses, she knew when her body was ready each month; even the tidal lock of her blood to her brother's.

Izzy's blood too, now. Tea could scent her following at a safe distance. Safe was good.

As she dug into the mutton that tasted like triumph, Tea suddenly realised she hadn't even thought of turning Izzy and Grant in to Mr MacGregor since that panicked run the night before. Dobbing them in would essentially be dobbing Robbie in, too, and she couldn't do that.

"Where d'ya think you're goin'?"

Dishes done, Mr MacGregor's bark caught Tea halfway down the veranda steps. She clasped her dirty, betraying hands behind her back and turned, having to look up and up to meet his gaze. He frowned. Was there *anything* that would please this man?

"Back to the cottage, if that's alright," Tea said as patiently as she could.

MacGregor's frown deepened. No, the boss wasn't about to allow her to relax.

"There's still daylight, girl. Daylight means work. Miss Twidle and Miss Atkinson are doin' their vegetable work." He flicked his head in the direction of the extensive gardens behind the house. "There's a fence down by the creek that needs mendin'. Jump to it, before some sheep decides to drown itself and we're down a few bob I might have to dock off your wages."

"But sir, Mr MacGregor, I—"

"You what, girl? Speak up. Don't want no lazy mumbling around here. Use your words, girl."

Tea's cheeks burned harder. That was what Mum said, and

the words always fled her under such scrutiny. She hated the impotence of her manner.

"I ... I don't know how to mend a fence, sir," Tea said, barely above a whisper. For everything else there'd been Izzy to show her, or she picked it up by copy-cat.

MacGregor huffed something that could have been a laugh, could have been disgust. The shape of Mrs MacGregor hovered at the washroom door.

"You knew well enough how to shear earlier."

"I can show her how," Grant said, stomping into his boots. "I know the break you mean. We can check the traps while we're down there, too."

Tea froze. She couldn't back out now without coming off a fool. MacGregor squinted at the sun, glanced to his wife, then scowled at the two young people. "Yer lucky that daylight saving's been made permanent. Make sure you're back before sundown. No shenanigans after dark, y'hear? Or ya both be out on yer ears, no pay."

He was looking hard at Tea. *What? Grant?* No, he was a nice boy, and useful in her letters back to Mum, but, *no!*

"You harness up Clarissa, I'll get the sled and tools," Grant said, veering off to the shed. Orders never sounded like orders from him.

Tea dragged her feet.

"You have a problem with that, girl?" MacGregor barked. A murmur came from the washroom, but he ploughed on. "Ol' Clarissa smell a bit too much for your delicate sensibilities, is it? We can always send you back home to Mummy if you like."

"No, sir. I mean, the smell is fine, sir. I was—" Tea bit her

49

lip. She'd almost gone too far, her tiredness making her tone slip.

"What is it, girl?"

Tell him, Robbie said somewhere in the back of her mind. "I was going to read."

"Read what?" MacGregor scoffed. "There were no letters for you in the post."

"No sir, I—"

That strange Virginia Woolf book Carmel and Alison had been giggling over all week teased at her mind. She'd tried to read it once before, but Mum had thrown it on the fire before she'd even read it a quarter of the way through. Grandad had been incandescent in his silent rage at the waste.

"The tractor manual, sir," Grant pitched in, halfway across the yard. Do mules have as good hearing as dogs? "I lent her the manual because I was going to teach her how to repair the tractor."

"Huh." MacGregor scratched his chin. He sized Grant up with that slow rake-over that still made Tea shiver. "All those technical terms might be a bit much for you, girl. But go ahead, try if you want."

With that he went back inside to his cup of tea. Her mouth dry, Tea wished she could have another, too.

Mrs MacGregor lingered a little longer on the veranda, watching them until they dipped below the hillock into the second paddock. Tea didn't need to look. The air did the shivering thing again as Mrs MacGregor moved it with her eyeballs and breath.

They were almost at the break along the creek, near the charcoal remains of the fire, before Tea could find her words again.

"Why did you do that?" came out in a rush, not at all the accusations and interrogations she had planned.

"I didn't lie to Mr MacGregor." Grant sounded as even as always, though he gave a little cough. "There is a tractor manual in your future."

"Stop it!"

Clarissa, nodding between them, thudded to a stop. Tea swore the Clydesdale sized them up. Would the placid old beast take Grant's side because of his equine-ness?

"Stop what?" Grant dragged the bag of tools off the sled. He could usually heft it fine, but it was the end of the day.

A very strange and trying day.

"Doing—" Tea waved a hand around. "Whatever it is you're doing. Pretending you're this."

"I'm not pretending anything," Grant said, laying out wire, hammer, nails. "I'm the same person I was yesterday."

"No, you're not!"

The heat flared up in Tea's head again. The hiss, one she now associated with the eels rushing and scraping against each other in a mad liquid dance, stretched her nerves further; a strange pulling of the breath from her lungs, a squeeze into the cracks of her mind, swirling instinct and her better intent into a whirl she didn't know how to contain. If Mum saw her now, there'd be a swift clip around the ear.

Anger is a man's place, this is a man's job. Grant and Izzy are trying to make me angry, make me into something I'm not!

Grant straightened and sighed, scratching under the rim of his hat. "Tea, come here."

"Why? So you can turn me into a horse too? Or a dog?" She

put the sheer size of Clarissa between them again.

"No. I need you to hold this wire so I can staple it into the post."

"Oh."

*

Prickle-sweet pine. Manure, settling dank and loamy at the back of the throat; the hardness of sheep pellets and oozing delight of cows' paddies. Sluggish ditches with worlds below thick water. The lick of green-yellow-sunshine grass-hay. Flea dip hard and high in the nose. Smooth-chewy lanolin over everything.

And her. The scent of her. Something old, and something new to this old place. Like the other one but deep-warm, sunshine on salt-sea-sand driftwood charcoal, the scent the river left in its wake a long time ago. The scent of what an eel thinks.

Whaiwhaiā.

Barely contained.

A lick of the chops, to wipe such a scent all over the face. To dig the nose in it, roll in it. Want to become a part of it. Take it all inside.

Tap tap tap. That is the hammer.

Is Clarissa one too? That is the voice, rough-sweet, smooth as river running over rocks.

One what? That is the other voice, round and long, a voice that waits.

Like you.

No. A laugh, a bray. *We do get on well because of commonalities.*

Common come on come one commonalities. Come all.

Like Izzy and the dogs.

Ears up, nose to the wind. Scent the dirt under fingernails, whisper from the creek, sweat. Come on.

Yes. Like you and all animals.

Yes yes. They like.

Taste-scent the hurt-fear how it rattles her skin and seizes her bones. Tiptoe around the deeper buried wild fruit that could over-ripen if not watched. Shake off the scrape-touch of the water reaching out for her. For *her*. Swallow jealousy.

What do you mean?

Watch your step there, the bank gets slippery under the ferns. I mean, the dogs, they like you. The chooks don't fight you or run away. The horses are placid around you, even the boss's Kingly. The sheep fair walk up and drop their fleeces for you.

That's silly!

You've never been on a farm before, have you?

Well, no? Woah there, Clarissa. Good girl.

Sunlight side-eyeing dust slanting up from the grass. Beyond, taste-scent of loam offering up the depth of its knowledge, a wealth of a thousand years. Ponga, flax, lemonwood, manakura, macrocarpa, and all the delicate morsels that make it their home. The fast-scent of feathers bob above, out of reach.

Bring her forward a bit more so the sled's hard up. Thanks.

Wait, what's that?

The traps. So, the dogs and horses, it usually takes them weeks to trust a new hand. You had them at first glance. Unh, this one's bogged down. Give me a hand, will you?

Slick mineral lick and longness of weed. Meaty rub against mud water stone air. The eels they come, they come when they should be away, away. Squirm squirm.

Yuck! Now my boot is wet!

It's alright. If you've oiled them properly, they should be waterproof. Ever had a pet?

No, Mum didn't like pets. Said they were bad for Grandad's lungs.

Hmm. Is your Grandad alright while you're on service?

He ... he passed. Just before the war.

I'm sorry.

Taste-scent of thick red, salt, hot meat, sweat. The mix is wrong, twists in ways that can't be unravelled. The air, it calls, close. Even at this distance she tastes she tastes she ...

Oh God! No! Let it out, stop it, put it back! No!

Auē. The wages of skin, they must be addressed.

*

The inky water let go its grip on the weed-draped cage. Blunt at one end and tapered with an inset cone at the other. Tea had never seen its like before, but instantly knew the death it brought.

Thick, rough whispers brushed her fingers as she hauled at the trap, some slapping like blame, others arching around in infinite coils of comfort.

A wet nose brushed her shoulder, then became hot breath against her ear whispering human words she couldn't – didn't want to – make out.

"It's not moving," Tea wept. "We have to send it back!"

Back to where she did not know. She should have *known*, what with the boss's talk of traps in the water, and memories of awful boys with sharp sticks and damp bags who tried to frighten her with oily eel faces, their bulbous lips and gnawing teeth. But to Tea they hadn't been ugly or scary. They simply belonged to the water, and the water belonged to them.

Larger hands engulfed hers, guiding her fingers to the hinges. Hunched in the mud, weeping, Tea cradled the dead eel in her hands. It was heavy, long, old, textured like fine sand. The coolness of it a reckoning, not the resistance that had sat ugly and coiled within her for so long. A resistance that nipped (*unladylike*), thrashed (*loud*), pushed and squirmed (*not marriage material*).

Unhuman.

The hand, again, gentle rough between her shoulder blades, a familiar comfort that hadn't been replaced since Grandad left.

A murmur-hiss of meaningless words, assurance from above and below the water.

We want the same want. We flow. Body here. Body in us. Body water beyond.

"They can't have them." Tea's voice hitched. Her tears mingled with the soft flowing creek, as was their right. She stroked the flaccid whiskers of the dead eel, but it wasn't creepy. It was skin she should know. "There's food enough. When *we* are hungry we are for our people." She knew she didn't mean *human*. "We can take each other inside when the time has come. Our hunger is ours. We will give willingly."

"We'll give it back, then. Tell Mr MacGregor the traps were empty."

Izzy's voice. Where had she come from? Her swoon lifting, Tea flinched away. Izzy must have come as her canine self. *Don't look!* A shiver coursed along Tea's skin at the glimpse of naked flesh.

"Yes," Tea murmured, holding the dead eel close, mindless of the slime and mud. "Give it back. That will do."

"Go on, then," Izzy urged, her bare arms wafting into view.

The sound rose in Tea's mind, the resistance now cut through. She made a *hsk hsk hsk* in the back of her throat, and the water roiled a welcome.

She lowered her hands in the water and sandy skin coiled around her wrists and fingers, flesh more pliant than she expected from their sinuous lengths. Mouths formed bubbles of surprise. Teeth gripped their companion, tearing and pulling it under, a grand feast. The same teeth nipped her fingertips but did not pierce. A thanks, a welcome, a commitment. Respect returned.

"Izz, look."

Tea brought her hands up into the almost-gone light dappling through the trees. Her tan skin melded at the wrists with thick, oily, black-green leather, the webs between her fingers elongated. Rubbing her hands together produced an approximation of the hiss that had held her all week. She closed her eyes. It felt like submerging her hands in the damp sand on a beach or running the fingertips across a thousand blades – one grain or tip would be an irritant or cut her, but all together the sensation made her vital, a spun strand of something bigger than herself.

When she opened her eyes again, the eel skin was gone, and her hands were normal. *No, not normal. Just human. This is the new normal now.*

"What am I?" Tea whispered, all the fight drained from her.

The eels thrashed around their meal, snapping the water with their tails. It sounded like gunshots in a far-off place.

"We're not going to hurt you," Izzy said softly. "We only want to help you understand. Become the best you."

"You're one of us now," Grant said, patting the patient Clarissa. The horse blinked.

Using the long fern fronds to her best advantage, Izzy was careful not to come into Tea's full view. Tea caught a glimpse of warm brown curves that made her curve in a little on her own.

They'd better move. The boss expected two, not three to return. How would Izzy get back to the cottage in this state? The water whispered reassurance; of course, she'd had a lot of practice.

"We three are tipua. We find strength in our animal forms. Our strength is whaiwhaiā. But you, Tea, are different. While Grant and I have forms that speak of the solidness of land, yours comes from the movement and change of water. You are taniwha."

The first two Māori words didn't mean anything, but the third spoke of something deep that had always been waiting. Tea wanted to flinch away, but the pressure of the water pressed her towards it. She caressed its sandpaper hide, the oily length of it. Here she was, in all her terrible glory.

Monster.

5.

Tea drowsed, letting Morgan carry her through the hissing, crackling day. The sun lulled her into a tranquillity that hadn't washed over her for weeks, months, years. She could almost forget a war was going on outside these hills. Or inside her skin.

She cracked an eyelid. Nothing but dogs huffing and shimmying around her ankles, sheep, brown grass, rocks protruding like bleached bones, and Izzy rocking gently in her saddle.

"How far now to the upper pasture?"

Izzy squinted at the sun. "Get out the map and compass. You tell me."

Tea frowned at the map. That tone of voice from Mum or Mr MacGregor put her back up immediately, but from Izzy, it made Tea dig deeper for the competence she expected from her.

A fly settled in her neck sweat, and she wriggled her shoulders to flick it off. No. It wasn't a fly, it was Izzy's contemplation. Why did she look at her like that?

Izzy jogged her horse, Carmine, over and reached to lay a tanned hand on the map, then pointed at a rock formation. "See that? That's there."

Tea measured it out with her fingers. Her hands were the same peachy sun-brown they had been when she left the farm that morning. No leathery scales creeping up her wrists, turning her into something she was not.

"Another four hours?"

"Sounds about right."

Tea licked her upper lip, and the tiny ripple of moisture grabbed her. Proximity to blood that moved like hers pulled her along without thought, poking along the rough edges of Izzy.

Izzy jumped and grinned at her, then reined Carmine around to whistle up a dog to chase down a wandering sheep. Tea tipped down her floppy hat to hide her blush and folded away the map.

That was careless. Everyone deserves their secrets.

That had sounded like Robbie's voice. She sometimes thought in his voice; what would Robbie do? But now, he sounded so close. This was the first time the voice had come through since that night at the creek. But how, with him so far away? When it had happened before, she always thought it was him whispering in another room or, when he wasn't around, her imagination.

Morgan grumbled, thirsty.

Tea shook up her canteen, shaking away the strange thoughts about her brother in her brain. "It's so dry out here."

"Then find us some water," Izzy called back.

"The next creek isn't until the mustering hut."

Izzy threw a look back over her shoulder Tea found hard to read. "What are you waiting for? The world is made up of water. Your body is water. Blood, piss, and everything else."

"Izzy!" Tea laughed. She'd never heard a girl swear before she came to the farm. So bad and so good at the same time.

Izzy pulled Carmine to a halt and waited for Tea to catch up. "If you're serious about your tipua, then you have to learn to work with it. I learned quick I couldn't ramble through life hoping it would all just happen. I didn't want to become a dog or show my real skin in the wrong situation."

Tea's neck prickled and shoulders tensed, a familiar reaction to criticism. Izzy was right, however. It was too dangerous to be herself.

"But I don't know what to do." Tea pulled Morgan around to bring a line of sheep back into place.

"You've got us. Me and Grant."

Tea flinched at the idea, but let it settle over her like the hot air.

Izzy kept on. "Grant, he's best with the ground beneath his feet. Me, I think it's the night air. For you, it's what happens when you touch the water. Those eels came to you. They're usually vicious little buggers, but they want to know you."

Tea took a deep breath. Earth, air, water. The elements. Did that make Robbie the fourth one, fire? "Alright. I'll try again."

"Good girl." It didn't sound condescending the way Mum or Mr MacGregor would say it.

Her eyelids lowered, sun-struck peach filtered through to show Tea shadows of the world moving around her. She focused on her skin and the sweat there, Morgan's tail a-whisk on the back of her legs. She let her hearing reach out to the cicadas creaking in the gorse bushes, their symphony growing louder as Tea imagined stroking her fingers through the water in the air.

Hisssssss.

Water nearby, slithering under the air's breath. Tea reached out to it, trying to pull on it, but something stuck in her chest, the hot day pulling the air from her lungs.

It was. Right. There. At the tip. Of her fingers. Whaiwhaiā. Burning cool as the water in the creek. A heat shimmer. But that block. An invisible shield. White as bone, white as the rocks.

HissssSSth.

The wriggle of sound taunted her flesh, tapping against her skull. The morning heat bristled. Wide as the open fields, high as the looming mountains. Points on a map, openings on her skin. Find the cracks in the veneer, the joins where she was *herself* and eelself. Long breath in through the nose. Open mouth. Stick tongue out. Lick the air. Suck in the taste-scent of skin, fur, dirt, wool … *Izzy*. Pulling down. Deep with each breath. Skin opening thirsty mouths. Teasing edge brushing fingertips, jaw, lips …

No. Tea shifted in her saddle, thighs taut. Stop reaching *that* way.

Hssssthssss.

Rocks. Earth. Grant might find his solidity in them, but to Tea's expanded senses they vibrated ever so gently, like the water was waiting, drowsing in its trap.

She poked at the idea of the rocks like a wound …

… then rocked back in her saddle as though she'd fallen face first into the ocean.

The *idea* of water flooded in, a jubilant sibilance. Streams *everywhere*. Along the sky, along the skin, along the ground, *under* the ground. Winding, pushing like blood in the veins, stretching out beyond her sight, reaching towards the ocean, then beyond … beyond all that …

Tea came to herself scrabbling in the bottom of a cut,

pushing aside rocks she couldn't have moved six months ago. Water pushed hard against stone beneath her hands, wanting out, wanting to be useful, wanting her praise. Wanting to take her to that beyond, where Robbie might be.

The water hesitated, afraid of the hot air turning it to nothing useful. Tea clenched her fists, then released them with a long outflow of breath. She *pulled* on the water like she had when she'd reached out to the eels, reeling in a rope made of silk, gentle, but firm enough to show love.

Izzy's triumphant whoop caused Tea to step back in time. The little stream flared out, searching for a way to join the river, greet Shag Point, caress the South Pacific, touch the Southern Ocean.

Around and around, all water is one.

"Look at what you did!" Izzy cheered, dancing on the spot as she held both Morgan's and Carmine's reins. Unimpressed, Morgan let go a stream of pee.

Tea shrugged her aching shoulders. "It's nothing."

"Nothing? You pulled water out of the ground like Jesus!"

"Izzy! Don't be blasphemous!" Tea couldn't help but glance around the empty valley. "How can this be a gift from God if there are only three of us that have it?"

"Four," Izzy reminded her, handing over reins and swinging back into the saddle. It took Tea three tries before she could make it up. "So, we don't know exactly where this comes from, but I *do* know it's something we need to make good use of."

That word again: useful. Bringing her back down to the ground again. She heard it in her mother's voice. What had she wanted, expected, from this? She hadn't thought much beyond the first panic coursing through her veins.

Wasn't this why she'd joined the land girls? To do something bigger while waiting and waiting and *waiting* for her brother to come home safe?

*

Panic rose in Izzy's chest like a full moon. She reached out to the mustering dogs as she tried to reach out to Tea with her words; the dogs had control, her tongue did not. The more she spoke, the further Tea retreated into her water-carved cave, but she couldn't stop.

"Imagine being able to find water even during the height of summer! We'd have the jump on the other farms. And you'd be able to touch the blood of lost animals. Less loss adjustment! And keeping the animals hydrated and the exact balance and time. Exact dipping and fertilisation, meaning less waste. Gosh, Tea. Your abilities are a gold mine for the farm!"

Maybe it was the wide-open space, being able to talk freely without the men looking down on her. Keeping herself to herself was so *hard*, even with Grant's quiet understanding.

Hours passed with Izzy's chatter falling like pebbles while Tea's face became stonier. Izzy poked around the edges of Tea's whaiwhaiā, but she didn't have the range the other girl did. She could get nothing off her. What had she said that made her lock up so tight?

The hills provided a welcome coolness as the sun crept lower and the mustering hut beckoned respite. Even dismounting, setting up the campfire, and restocking the little tin hut, Izzy couldn't stop her mouth running wild.

"I'm doing this for Robbie."

The dam burst, and words fell out of Tea like rushing water. "I'm doing this for Robbie. All the boys can go off to war, but we can't!"

Suddenly fumbling for words, Izzy stripped a saddle bag off Carmine with fumbling fingers. She'd never seen Tea this stormy. It didn't feel right at all. "It's not what women are supposed to do."

"Forget *supposed to*," Tea enunciated slowly as she curried Morgan down. "What about fair? Shouldn't the world be fighting with every tool at its disposal? Aren't women useful beyond looking after the land and the kitchen?"

Izzy sighed and leaned her forehead against Carmine's sweaty flank. Fighting. Anger. Fists. She wasn't allowed to show them. Her tongue like a knife, maybe, when the moment was right. But she couldn't betray herself, her blood, like that. And neither should Tea.

"I know it's not ladylike." Tea's voice swelled with waves of emotion. Her anger was a flood. "But I can't be part of this war and be expected to keep smiling all the time!"

"You're going too fast, Tea. I know it's not fair. It's horrible, and I want to make it better for you, for all of us girls left behind. But you need to learn how to use your whaiwhaiā, and how to temper it." Izzy couldn't bring herself to look Tea in the eye. "You can't go full tit, or you'll burn out. It will hurt you." She started to say more, but she bit it back.

"What do you mean? How could something so special hurt me? This isn't a cold or a cut. It's not an illness that would … would kill …" She trailed off for a moment, hand clenched in

Morgan's mane. "I have to *do* something."

The fight, the stone, in Tea's voice made Izzy flinch. "I've never heard you speak like that. That you wanted to fight."

"It's not a very ladylike thing to mention."

"Bugger ladylike! We're up to our elbows in sheep shit daily."

"Izzy!"

Long shadows from the hills touched their feet. Yes, this was what she was good at. Izzy reached into the shadow, twisted it to her means. There. Anger taste. Whaiwhaiā burning too bright, too hard, too loud.

"Tea, show me your hands."

"Huh? Why?"

"Take your gloves off." Izzy had to take a deep breath. The shadow was squeezing her chest. "Please."

Tea stripped off her leather riding gloves. "See. Dirty, from being up to our elbows—"

Izzy dropped the handful of grass she was using to brush Carmine and grabbed Tea's hands. Tea flinched at the sudden touch.

"This is what I'm talking about." Izzy squeezed Tea's hands too hard, making knuckle grate painfully against knuckle.

The skin on Tea's hands up to the tan line was darker than the rest of her. Not quite the oily taniwha skin of that incredible, terrible first night of discovery, but the scale ridges were showing.

Izzy continued. "If you're not practised, if you're not careful, things will start to show. Then you'll really be in trouble. If you want to fight, you have to *survive* first. Do you *know* what they do to people like us? They call us mad. Lock us away in asylums. Put us in prison. And they don't do it to protect us. They do it to protect themselves. They just don't know from *what*."

Tea stared at her hands, and the hands holding her. The war, inside and out, battled across her face.

"Concentrate," Izzy said, weariness weighting her grip. "You have to learn to concentrate. Carry on. Chin up. Pay attention. All those things we hate to hear."

Tea pulled away, rougher than she should have, her ragged nails scratching Izzy's flesh lightly. In the moment it took her to turn back to attending Morgan, her features moved like heat against the hills. Her skin rougher, a shimmer of oily colour. Hair like tendrils. Her desires a halo. Then she was Tea again, rounded cheeks, pert, tired.

Izzy couldn't bear the taut silence in which they set the fire, billy, and stew pot. Muttering something about checking the sheep, she drew space around her and paced the long line of the flock. Twilight and exuberant dogs danced around her as she tried to sort through the detritus of her thoughts. Had she pushed her friend too far?

Friend. She was thinking of Tea as a friend. But it was more, much more than that. Something people called unnatural. Something she had been far more afraid of than her canine flesh. Being a dog was easy. Being human, her type of human, was almost impossible.

She had to be careful there, too.

The day's wariness and weariness settled into her bones and muscles. The fire was so inviting, but she didn't want to encroach on Tea's space and thoughts. Stars prickled overhead, the celestial shapes of her ancestors. Did Robbie look upon these same stars, too, and think of home?

Robbie. Was he holding a gun, driving a tank, building a bridge? What did a sapper do, anyway? She found it easier to imagine him building something rather than destroying, bringing death.

*

Tea massaged her right hand. How could she have been so careless, not even realising her eelskin was growing on her under her gloves? Another thing she had to learn now she was on her own. Robbie had always been the last one to see her leave the house, or she'd look in a mirror. She'd hated and loved her brother's fussing, thought herself vain.

Released from saddle stance, the pain in her right arm grew, little spasms shivering her bicep, her elbow stabbing like it was full of hot glass. She clenched and opened her right hand, stretching her fingers wide, but nothing made the pain dissipate. It was like the creek hadn't let her go, like it had wrapped its eel tails around her hand and was pulling, pulling …

"You alright there?" Izzy's voice, out of the nearby dark.

"Uh. Don't creep up like that. You scared me." Tea hugged her upper arms, where goosebumps had replaced the almost-scales on her skin.

"Sorry. I thought you heard me." Izzy's face resolved into angles underlit by the fire.

"Mmm, no. Too lost in my thoughts again. Not being careful enough."

"Tea, I need to apologise. I was too harsh—"

"No, you're right. Maybe it was … instinct."

"Preservation."

"Yes." Tea clenched her hand again, the hot stabs unrelenting. She tried to put a wan smile on her face. She hated Izzy being mad at her.

"Thattagirl. Hey, what's up with your arm?"

"I don't know. Saddle cramp, probably."

"Let me look."

The scent of Izzy's skin being slightly *wrong* made Tea flinch back. "No! You've still got fur on you. And you changed when you told *me* not to!"

"So? No-one out here but us. And I don't bite. Well, not hard."

"But we were just talking about …"

"Yeah. I know. Sorry about that, mate. Maybe you should let your skin go, for a bit. Sometimes it's nice to relax."

Tea still didn't give her hand over to Izzy's investigations. "Are we mates?"

"Of course." Izzy bit her lip, her eyes slipping away for a moment. "Look, I'm sorry for being so harsh. Really. That's my preservation instinct. Things are … harder for us." Izzy patted a dog that nuzzled her as if in agreement.

The heat now reached Tea's eyes, and she knuckled away the dampness it created there. "Why is this happening to me?"

"What, the whaiwhaiā? It's not *happening* to you, it's your power. It's what *you* do with *it*."

"Don't tell me it's a gift or I'll … ow!" A quake of resistance travelled up and down Tea's arm.

"What did I say before? You're trying too hard."

"No. That wasn't me. It's like someone punched me in the arm."

"Hmm. Like that time at the dinner table."

"That was a wasp … oh, bother it. I know it wasn't. Yes, like that, but it's becoming more intense."

Tea screwed up her face, trying to remember all the sensations of that first night. In the light of discovering Grant and Izzy's whaiwhaiā, she'd considered and dismissed it as one of them giving her a metaphorical 'kick', but they didn't have the connection to water like she did. "It comes and goes. I just … *know* it's not connected to the eels or my skin. It's something different again."

"This has happened before?" Izzy wriggled her fingers in a *gimme* gesture, and Tea finally relented. Somehow Izzy's hands were hard and soft at the same time. "Why didn't you say something?"

"I thought it was just me getting used to the heavy workload."

Izzy massaged Tea's knuckles, rubbing her hands between her palms like rubbing a dowel to start a fire, except the effect was cool relief trickling along her nerves. "There. That's better. Hey look, your eelskin is coming in, nice and smooth. Well done."

"Ow!" Tea pulled her hands out of Izzy's grasp, strange relief clashing with the throbbing pain. "You said it would stop if I turned a little."

"I said it would help you relax. Here. Let me put a cold rag on it." Izzy squeezed out a rag in the bucket of water they'd collected for cleaning. "There. That better?"

"Not really, but thank you." Tea hoped Izzy couldn't see her blush in the low light.

"Has this strange pain happened before you came to the farm?"

"Hmm. I don't know." A memory intruded, dribbling heat back into the well created by the coolness. Tea caught her breath, her chest tight. "Well … no. That's silly. I'm making it up."

"No. Go on. Tell me. Nothing you tell me can be stranger than what we already are."

"Well. Oh gosh. Robbie used to get into fights when he was out at dances. I somehow … knew before he got home. To be ready to clean him up. Like I felt the blows, too." She bit her lip, tears threatening to embarrass her again. "If it was bad then, when he was close by, what is happening to him that I can feel it a world away?"

Izzy's expression twisted into something Tea had never seen on her mother: a sharing of pain, a creating of space to let her feelings for Robbie sit and be nourished. She loved her twin more than she'd ever been allowed to admit, and now this. She'd pushed it away too long. They were connected by more than just familial ties.

The weight of Izzy's gaze became too great, and Tea looked away. "Pass the tea, please."

"Tea. Look at me," Izzy pleaded. "You have to know what's going on."

"I do. I can't …"

"I know Robbie. We've worked together. We're friends."

How can women and men be friends like that? Madness from the pain clashing and chewing on Tea's thoughts. *They're supposed to get* married *if they like each other …*

Izzy continued, "There's this thing. When we're in our animal skin. We can … reach out to each other. And it makes sense you'd feel Robbie much stronger because you're linked by blood."

"By water. That storm Grant talked about." Lightning struck along Tea's veins. "OW! Oh, bother it. That one really stings."

"Tea, he's at war—"

The tears were running freely down Tea's cheeks now, the pain fluid, running all over her like the flow of the river. "I know," came out as a strangled whisper. "He's in battle. That's what I can feel, isn't it? I don't know what to do. He's all the way over there. I'm here."

"You're doing the best you can, fighting the good fight on the home front."

"Don't give me that propaganda!" Tea twisted her hands together like she wanted to break the bones to make the pain empty out of them. "I bet girls could fight and still be ladies, given half the chance."

The dark hand of pain had worked around her neck and up her skull.

"Oh Tea. Here's your, er, tea …"

A small moan was the only thing that could escape Tea's frozen face.

"Tea? Tea! What's going on? Tea! Oh, sh—"

Sky, land, and the water in between all smashed together in a furious chaos full of shooting stars and darkness black and crumbling as coal. The grind of muscle against skin, flesh against bone, blood through veins, the pulse of her heart filling her mind until she thought that was all she ever could and would be. The pounding sped up, slowed down, then she almost strangled on the silence. Her heart tripped over and started again.

Kick. Flesh in spasm. Knuckles cracking. Bones twisting back on themselves. Skin, like a thousand needles, shaping her to its will. A voice, but Tea couldn't make out any words. It was deep and rough like a man's, then higher and slower like a woman's.

Shouts, muffled and distant, as if hearing them through wind and rain. A rattle, pennies in a tin. Stars exploding in languid arcs, ice-burn fragments sizzling through her edges.

She tried to stand, but her legs wouldn't answer her call. She could only see staccato night.

And the pain in her arm! Hot and cold and fierce and she wanted to tear it from her, grow another, grow a different *her* ...

Tea seeped back into herself, the light-dark chaos receding into a half-remembered nightmare. Her chest ached, as though her heart had almost succeeded at hammering its way out.

"There you are." Izzy's voice, warm and gentle. "You were gone a long time."

Tea tried to speak, but only an eel-like hiss came out. She was lying down, her head on something soft and warm.

Izzy's lap.

Izzy's onyx eyes held her pinned down. Beautiful, so different to Grant's guarded green gaze. Tea tried to pull away, but it only manifested as a frustrated twitch. No. Women don't look at other women like that. It was *wrong*.

Maybe Izzy was concerned. Yes, that's it.

"I'm fine." Tea's voice slurred like she'd had too much sherry after dinner.

Izzy helped her sit up. A relief not to be held in that strange way, but Tea also felt the loss of her warmth. "No, you're not. That was something altogether different from the incident down at the creek. Where did you go?"

Tea tested out her arm. It held only a memory of pain now. "I think … I think I was in a battle."

"With who? Where?"

"There was sand. And it was night. And the stars. No, they must have been bullets and shells. And the shouting. And the water there. Tastes so different. My arm hurt so much. But it doesn't now. Oh, that all sounds a mess. I'm not making any sense at all."

Izzy took her arm and searched for eelskin, but it had gone. She tested Tea's muscles with her strong fingers, and the pressure felt good. Tea had never been touched by boys – a dance here, an elbow on the way home there – but this …

"You went to the war," Izzy said softly before letting Tea's arm go. Cool night rushed in to fill the void left by her touch.

Tea's hands shook as she took up a mug of tea. "I think I was near Robbie. I was feeling his pain. Something is wrong with his arm. I don't know if he's injured. Just … his arm doesn't feel the right *part* of him. Oh, that doesn't make sense at all."

"The whaiwhaiā is strong between the two of you."

The word *magic* burned sour as Tea took another sip of the bitter brew. "Grant says a storm is coming, and I think I felt part of that now. But I don't know what any of it means, or what I'm supposed to *do* with it. I'm here, Robbie's there. There are oceans between us."

Izzy rubbed the ears of a sleeping dog acting as a pillow. "Perhaps that's it. Water is everywhere. Your lingering power from that tapped into something that was happening to Robbie, and he was near a strong body of water …" she stopped, shook her head. "I can only guess. We need to talk to Grant. But I think he'll agree with me. We all have a lot of work to do. You have to practise your water thing—"

"My eelskin."

"Yes, if that's what you want to call it."

Izzy didn't laugh. Izzy wasn't afraid of her. Izzy didn't treat her like the girls at school, the girls on the street. Izzy *heard* her words and gave them the weight they deserved.

"I … I'm scared, Izzy."

An arm slid back around Tea's shoulders. How could something so wrong be so right? But it was only them here. Izzy with her scent of starlight, her breath sharing her water from deep within.

"It's alright, Tea. We'll figure it out. Whatever happens, we'll do it together. Promise me you won't go doing something foolish if the call comes through … through the—"

"The water."

"Yes, through the water, and you hear it first. Promise you'll wait for us."

"I promise."

Together. Us. Whaiwhaiā. The words smelled like a home Tea had never known.

6.

Christmas, 1942.

The best present Tea could receive was relief from the strange pain. It didn't entirely dissipate – lingering in her skin as a scratchy memory, exacerbated by the oncoming heat like a rash – but further medicine came in a letter from the front. Robbie could not write about what he'd been through, due to censorship rules, but it was enough to know he was safe, alive, and grumbling about sunburn.

Spring lambing had bled into a brittle summer, the grass turning brown almost overnight. The heat radiated from the hard North Otago soil and crunching grass, brush fires hiding in wait. The hot Nor'wester blasted the senses and pushed dust into everything. The dogs barked at nothing, putting Izzy on edge. Sometimes she'd crawl into her dogskin at night to share a blanket in the dog runs to keep them quiet. A dangerous thing to do, but Izzy told Tea she'd had plenty of experience slipping in and out of form near other people, and the MacGregors were creatures of habit.

The sheer weight of the work never let up. The girls went to bed exhausted every night. Though Tea groaned to Izzy about her aches and pains, excessive expectations from the boss, and the sharp tongue and eye of Mrs MacGregor, a growing sense of achievement pervaded her discomfort. She was *doing* something!

Underneath it all, water seethed. Even when she was dead tired from a day of fencing, dagging, hoeing, chopping, riding, docking and dipping, mucking, wool sales, counting feed, manipulating heavy ploughs head-down in the wind, fertilising, fixing, and generally making do, even when the Nor'wester blasted around the edges of the cottage and she tried to read her books and letters by lamplight, she strained to touch the hiss of the creek.

A low-level itch took up in her hands that had nothing to do with trimming gorse or pulling Old Man's Beard. She too used the cover of dark to pull at her new skin, taking sips of lukewarm water from a chipped cup and practising flipping scales up and down her forearms. It didn't always happen. She could never tell when her whaiwhaiā would respond, whether the water would take or give. The weather and her weariness had nothing to do with it. Frustration was a constant friend.

The early morning Christmas Eve train back to Dunedin was packed with girls in wool uniforms too thick for the enclosed space, gritty wind rocking the carriages. Tea's full uniform had arrived in November, and unwrapping the brown paper package had felt as much like early Christmas as Robbie's letter. The jauntiness of her pinned hat brim made her hold her head up. Some other girls had to look twice at the Land Service epaulet, and Tea bit her lip to manage her grin. The name had only changed recently, as if Land 'Army' was too strident for girls. Though the chocolate brown uniform didn't sport as many gleaming buttons and badges as the other corps, its refined lines brought her close to feeling a kinship with other girls that she hadn't before. She could hide her broken and dirty fingernails inside her gloves.

The only Māori girl in her carriage was wearing Women's Auxiliary Army Corps khaki – *They were allowed to serve there?* Tea wondered – gave Tea a single, knowing look, then ignored her for the rest of the trip.

Dunedin. Home. An abstract idea she had to stitch back together from a patchwork of memories that even after only a few months away didn't come together seamlessly.

The place where Mum was. Where Robbie wasn't. Where Grandad wasn't anymore. Where her father had never been.

With a little time and space in her head between *here* and *there*, she chewed over thoughts of her father as the train clicked past glimmering Seacliff, headed across the lagoon from Warrington, and then puffed uphill from Waitati.

It was hard to miss someone you never knew. His shadow had sprung into her thoughts more often in the last few months than any other time in her life. A shadow as large as the fire in her blood.

Peter Gray. His name meant little. Tea had never known that side of her family, other than they lived 'way back country'; Mum said this with the same inflection as 'them mowrees'. Maybe that wasn't his real name at all. Mum would never tell her how they met. There was no photo of him in his Great War uniform. Tea didn't even have a whisper of a memory of him. He'd gone to war not long after she and Robbie had been born.

The very few Māori girls Tea had known before Izzy – at school, down at the shops, or the groups that stuck together as they left the factories – kept to themselves. The girls at school had whispered about them, the size of their noses, the black thickness of their hair, their drab clothes. Did they take their cottons off and put on their grass skirts as soon as they got home? Did they really run around taunting men with their bare chests, wild eyes, and long, sticking-out tongues?

Tea had often assessed the angle of her jaw, the wideness of her nostrils. Was her nose as big as theirs? Izzy could pass easily as white. Tan, but not too tan, stout, but still slim, like a good, healthy Kiwi girl.

Mum met Tea at the train station. Moments after she greeted her, she was annoyed by the venting steam engine, the excited voices bouncing off stone, and the temperature being so high for early morning. Not much had changed for Tea's mother in the months she'd been away.

The walk up the hill didn't steal Tea's breath like it used to, and she was glad for the firm, sensible grip of her uniform shoes. Mum said nothing about her sharp ensemble, instead chattering about letters from Robbie. Had Tea received any she would like to share?

Christmas Day came and went in blessed quiet, with the small piece of lamb Mrs MacGregor had given her roasting in the range. Without Robbie there to supervise, the tree sat forgotten in the bay window, paper chains haphazardly looped. The quiet of prayer in between the thunder of the church organ, fewer people in between the concrete walls to soak up the sound. Mum smiling at her gift of handmade doilies, while Tea didn't quite know what to make of the package of lacy handkerchiefs she gave her.

Tea had saved up all her rations for chocolate, but the doilies had been a last-minute decision. They were a little clumsy after months of not touching hook and cotton. Frilly wasn't Grant or Izzy's style. She gave them the chocolate instead.

After the bottle of cooking sherry made an appearance, Mum's words came out as clipped as the holes in Robbie's letters. They read and shared, but beyond a cheeky mention about Robbie 'purchasing a pair of lady's silk stockings' which Mum claimed not to understand with an uncharacteristic blush, there was nothing they could discover of his whereabouts. And that suited Mum fine. To her, Robbie was safe, well behind the lines, building bridges or laying train tracks. Working hard like a good boy should.

The ache in Tea's fingers told her otherwise.

The ache was covered up the next day as she plunged her hands into buckets of hot water and clenched her fingers around rag and scrubbing brush. The next part of her Christmas present, Mum explained, was a tea party with all her church friends and their girls before they headed back to base. Tea couldn't think of anything worse to do on her last day of furlough.

"You need to get those elbows into some proper, decent work," Mum said as Tea set to on the living room floor. "I can't imagine what you'll do out there with all that time on your hands once you've finished the gardening, pickling, and bottling."

Tea had to bite her lips shut over a retort about where Christmas dinner had come from.

The next day, the teacups rattled with talk of likely service lads and the mock cream shivered with whispers of station bicycles. Izzy had explained the term to a shocked Tea. "But the farmer tends to go to the girls' cottage, not the other way round as townies seem to think," Izzy said, her eyes narrow and dark. Tea didn't want to ask what she meant. When Izzy sounded angry, you didn't want to get in the way.

The girls in snappy Women's Royal Naval Service or Auxiliary Air Force blue smiled at Tea, pleasant enough in the sight of their mothers, but Tea found herself more often than not with a plate of scones or the teapot in her hands, doing the rounds. The implication was easy to infer: the girls in blue had attained some higher status than someone in simple land brown. Meat and wool, vegetables and fruit were important to keep the country going, but Land Girls were not invited to march or wave a flag. It was in their name: service.

Tea smiled, murmured Grant's name in appropriate places, served scones, and kept her stocking seams straight. And when her edges were raw, when the heat became too much, she reached out to the slither of the nearby stream and drew on its gentle strength.

By the end of furlough, she was proud not to have slipped into her eelskin once, not even in her dreams.

Her joy at wearing her uniform in public dissipated the moment she arrived back at the farm and Mrs MacGregor had her back in work clothes. There was fruit rotting on the trees while she had lolly-gagged in the city.

So much for her life being more than jam jars and big pots of stewed fruit.

From sickly sweet to sweetness – Izzy and Grant, delighted at their Christmas gifts, had saved the chocolate to share.

The winds of December became the long dry heat of January,

cicadas shrieking from dawn to dusk. Sunburn gave way to a smattering of freckles. A change to her skin that was normal and real. Mum had said a work-day face would be a hard sell to a potential husband after the war, but the word 'husband' didn't send a frisson through Tea like it had a year ago. She didn't know why. She didn't want to.

The few days back in the city had shown Tea how little she had come to mind the grit and muck. Her biceps and thighs had taken on a solidity she took secret pleasure in, measuring them with her fingers in the dark. They kept her upright and going with purpose. Sometimes she thought she caught Izzy staring at her muscles, like the way Izzy had looked at her that strange night up at the mustering hut, but when she looked again those dark eyes were elsewhere.

Her thoughts about her father, the ones she thought she had put away after Christmas, jumbled together when caught off guard by a casual reminder from the MacGregors. Mr MacGregor groused about "some mowree caught stealing" on another farm, and Mrs MacGregor complained about "that lazy wah-hee-knee at the shop". They pronounced place names with a hard smack or swallow: "Tie-ree", "Why-koo-white", "Carry-tane", "Om-ah-roo" – quite unlike Izzy's rolling roundness spoken in private.

Tea had been lulled by the gentle push of water from the creek and her strengthening flesh, so these reminders of what her skin, her whaiwhaiā, could take away from her were like punches. She practised only in the dark or in the shade of the creek. The eels mouthed against her fingers – *come in, the water'ssss fine* – and her scales flickered oily and sleek, the boil in her blood like low-banked coals.

*

Summer ebbed and flowed into autumn with the crackle of brush fires and the clipped, cheerful-serious tones of the BBC. Mr MacGregor let the girls listen to the wireless when he was out at Home Guard or farmer's association meetings, or after dinner if they remained absolutely quiet with their sewing. Izzy found it hard to remain so still, but at least managed to stay for a full bulletin or play, for Tea's sake. Tea couldn't parse much of what the news reader said, and often excused herself due to weariness. Place names like Egypt, Syria, and Turkey, she had to look up in her atlas, but she could draw no shape or meaning that she couldn't get out of the shivers and spasms from her arm and the growing restlessness of the water.

The creek did not ache down to a summer trickle.

March marched right on into the farm. Leaves turned a scintillating red and yellow. Winter feed stacked. Fields turned over to sit fallow. More wood chopped to keep the homestead and cottages running. Alison often complained about Tea's jerky sawing motion. Tea brushed it off as weariness and Alison bought the excuse easily, disgusted. Though she tried her best with Alison and Carmel, the girls held to their wariness. Like they felt something about her, her fire, but couldn't put their finger on it.

Tea's exhaustion sprung from the deep ache that woke her in the night.

As March grew late, the sensation didn't abate, settling into a dull throb that came and went like a tide. Though she thought the burden of her pain connection to her brother was hers to bear, she often saw flickers between the other two, like lightning between the clouds. Swift, hard, sharp, but gone in an instant. Grant in the yards or fields rubbing his joints like an arthritic. Izzy, usually staunch, complained of pain in her elbows.

Tea hid her pain. It took the last of her energy not to rush down to the creek and plunge her hands into the cool water, or keep her eelskin from turning at inappropriate moments. Her dreams became fretful and dark. She often woke with her fingers webbed and black. It took her longer for her human flesh to return from its slippery state, pulling hard on the hiss-feel. The hiss pulled right back.

*

"Come on, girl. Cows to milk. Upsy-daisy."

Tea groaned. Her fingers were a normal tan-brown as she flipped over the calendar to Saturday, March the twenty-seventh.

Her arm settled into its daily ache.

"Oh, Bess. Stop being such a pest!" Tea slapped the rump of the fractious cow. "Give it up, there's a good girl."

"That's the third time Clover has stood on my toes!" Izzy yelped. Her bucket clattered, and she gave an unladylike curse.

"When you girls have finished mucking around in there, that butter won't churn itself," Mr MacGregor bellowed. "And don't forget rabbit cull starts this afternoon. We need all hands on deck."

"Yessir!" they chorused.

In her mood, Tea decided, handling a gun would be just the thing. Mr MacGregor had grumbled about girls learning to shoot and handle the ferrets, but, as in everything, they were short-handed, and they couldn't skip rabbit cull. The skins brought in good extra money. Three of the horses had almost been lamed by holes in the fields, more than enough sheep had been lost to broken legs, and there was damage to feed stock.

As they stalked through the thistles that forever needed grubbing and the gorse that scoured her skin, Izzy's dark glances clawed at the surface of Tea's patience.

"Stop it," she hissed out the corner of her mouth. Spotting movement, she loaded, shouldered, and popped off. The rabbit dropped, but with the kickback of the rifle, the pain in Tea's shoulder increased. *Good God, if Mum knew I was using a rifle …*

"Stop what?" Izzy demanded once the boom-ring of the shot died down.

"You're staring at me. Like I'm about to … turn into something."

"What bee you got in your bonnet? You on the rag?"

Tea blushed. "What if I am?"

"Your blood is up. Thought so." Those canine senses of hers!

They picked up some dropped rabbits, and Tea stomped back to the dray to empty her sack into the bloody morass. The stink helped maintain the potency of her mood, ignore the pinch and flutter of her bicep. She should apologise. Izzy was a good friend but for some reason today the thought of how easily she could slide in and out of her fur annoyed Tea no end.

A scratch against her skin. Dry. With the stench of iron and salt. Not the fullness of her menses or the softness of the creek. More … something that wasn't of *here*.

"Hey." Izzy's soft interjection made Tea jump. She tilted her head like an inquisitive dog, and the words settled across her mind. *Something's happening, isn't it?* "Making sure you're alright."

"I'm fine," Tea snapped, unable to stop the words. "I'm not a baby. You're not my mother. I take care of myself."

She sounded like …

… *sounded like Robbie.*

Yes. Izzy was definitely in her head.

Tea squeezed her eyes shut, clenched her fist, and flinched again at a spasm in her arm. Thank goodness the rifle pops from MacGregor and the other girls came from another field beyond a stand of pines.

"Robbie would sound like that—"

"—when he came back from dances. I know."

Izzy tilted her head the other way. "Dances?"

"He used to get in a lot of fights. Over girls."

A small, sad smile hooked at the corner of Izzy's mouth. "Oh, Tea."

A crack-crack. Tea jerked her head towards the sound.

But there was no-one with rifles that way.

Rattle-crack.

No rifles that way either.

Blackness seethed around the edges of Tea's vision. She held tight to the edge of the dray to stop herself from falling. The darkness boiled like thrashing water. Water against stone. Tide rolling over. Waves sweeping away, damn whatever was in its way.

"Tea. Izzy."

A voice in the here and now. Grant. He never yelled, not even at the animals. But the cut of his voice held stone in it, the heaviness of earth.

"Tea?" Izzy's voice had that growl, like she was right on the edge of change, too restless for her skin.

Both voices slurred through air that had thickened around Tea's head. She tried to shake herself free of the strange grip. The effort to breathe exhausted her.

Two pairs of hands gripped her arms, took the rifle from her.

"It's here … it's here …"

"What is, Tea?" Izzy asked.

"That storm," Grant said. "Tea can feel something going on, over there. But I told you, the dust …"

"That's your sneezes."

"Be fair, Izz. I might not be as strong as Tea or you or … or Robbie, but I know when things aren't right."

"My arm … Robbie's hurt …"

"My hand has been giving me heck all day, Izz."

"You shouldn't be able to feel it at this distance."

"Tea can."

"What are you talking about? You can feel … the storm, the fight, that Robbie's in?"

"It's not just the war."

"Grant, shush. Now isn't the time. What do we do?"

"Get her to the creek. I'll meet you there. I'll … tell Mr MacGregor the dogs spooked a wild boar and we're going to track it. He won't say no to the meat."

"Right oh. Up you go, girl. Come on."

"Izz. It hurts!"

"I know, girl. Hold on, we're almost there."

"The fire … can't hold it in …"

"Oh, shoot … Robbie, why now? Here we go. Down here. That's a good girl, Clarissa, you old tough nut."

"Ow … hurry, they're calling me!"

"Who?"

The *hisssssth* of the water wove a torrent around Tea's head. Slippery strands like seaweed in the weave, gripping her hands and pulling her under. Heavier things called and pulled from further away and deep, cold flow hot flow, great walls of viscosity rubbing against each other, the *hisssssth* sensuous, angry, always moving, always *alive* and teeming, boundless, skin bones blood mettle all part of it.

"There's sand. Lots of sand. And salt. Salt in the wounds. It burns. So cold. Shooting stars. No, that can't be right. Not that many. A river. River salt red. Blood. Oh God, the blood!"

She came out of her daze up to her elbows in the creek, the eels nibbling reassurance and wrapping love around her wrists. *Come swim come*, they whispered. Her own eelskin flipped fast and black up her arms.

Grant burst through the bushes, more energetic and precise than Tea had ever seen. He looked like a show horse ready to jump rails rather than the steady donkey he kept in check. His right hand clenched in a familiar spasm.

"You feel it," Tea gasped, wiping a scaled hand across her loose lips, then plunging it back in the water as soon as the sting gripped her again.

"It's Robbie. He's in a fight. A battle." He shook his head when Tea frowned. "And things are going—"

"—wrong. Very wrong," Tea finished.

How did Grant feel Robbie's pain this strongly? He wasn't connected by blood like her. She glanced around the muddy bank and bushes as if searching for an answer. Her gaze skittered over Grant; anger and fear made an uncomfortable mix in the usually steady boy. Izzy stood as solid as the rock she had always been, only her fingers twitching. Dogs danced with agitation, and Clarissa shifted from hoof to hoof. Maybe the whaiwhaiā was so powerful something was leaking off her. If the animals were picking it up, why not another human?

The words fell out of Tea's mouth before the thought formed fully in her head. "I have to go to him."

"Go where? How?"

Tea's fingers caught in the laces of her boots. Undressing; another involuntary response. And in front of a boy, no less! "I'm ... I'm going to swim there."

"I'm coming, too." Izzy bent to undo her own boots, as if this idea made perfect sense.

Grant flushed – fury or embarrassment, or both. "Tea, maybe. She's a taniwha." His pronunciation was terrible: 'tanny-farr'. "But you're canine, and I'm ... well, I can't *ride* across oceans!"

He spoke as if he believed Tea could make it.

Sssssswim come sssssshow you.

Being this close to the creek's agitation, its *depth* and *breadth*, pulled the breath from Tea's lungs. Its song itched at her until she wanted to tear all her flesh off to reveal her eelskin beneath.

"Wait here."

Something in the tone of her voice made Izzy and Grant pause.

Tea waded out in the creek. She thought it would only come up to hip or chest height. She went under spluttering when within three steps the bottom of the creek dropped away to nothing.

With a swirl of kissing black skin, the eels roiled around her, holding her up, pushing her forward.

Swim.

Tea thrashed for the surface, all stars and knives of light. She'd never been the strongest swimmer and her lungs ached for breath.

Come.

An especially large and tenacious eel circled her chest and squeezed.

Bubbles from her terrified screech shot up but the water did not rush in to kill her. The eels demanded something of her bones, her muscles, her breath until it all creaked and cracked and she felt as long as all the rivers combined and as wide as the oceans.

She was not Tea anymore. She was a hiss of a beast, lengthened out into something finer and truer. The age-old water song promised her a might her human flesh could never imagine.

Her eelskin tasted, sinuous eeltongue smelled, and eelsight heard in a series of rumbles and shifts, a gargle-rattle of a thousand throats all singing different hymns but the same song, the water song. And within that song, disharmony; water shed, breath shed, bloodshed.

A border approached, where the green loam of the creek met sharp mineral. Creek to the ocean to the currents that swirled and touched and loved and mixed and broke apart again, delivering song sweetness savour surrender to the other side. Tea touched this border with wispy protrusions; she had to cross over to get *there*.

Beyond *there* was Robbie, caught in the tornado of danger battle blood death.

What remained of her human mind cried out *I can't do this! I'm not a fighter! I'm only a girl.*

Sssswim come eelgirl squirmed the water and eels. *Ssshow you like we ssshow all.*

Show all? Show who?

No time.

I have to do this. I must. For Robbie. Even if it hurts. Even if it kills me.

Tea gave herself over to the current. The water gave itself over to her. Fight, pull back, move around, *hold*. A merging, as water and water should.

The wisps around her resolved into long, thick whiskers, extensions of her eel flesh. Anything would be safe wrapped in their embrace.

She rose to the surface.

Gasps from Izzy and Grant.

"Is it that bad?" Tea found her words coming out round and deep from an elongated mouth and long chest. "Am I a hideous beast?"

Grant's large Adam's apple bobbed in his scrawny neck.

Izzy stared, eyes as soft as a moonless night. "No," she said. "You are beautiful."

7.

"Dragon," Izzy argued, fists on hips.

"Mermaid!" was Grant's rebuttal.

"But the whiskery things, and scales!"

"No wings, though. No fangs and claws, either. And look at that tail!"

"Do fairy tales ever talk about a black mermaid? No. And that's just what they are. Tales. Tea is very much real. I think she's more dragon."

"And I say mermaid!"

In Tea's new peripheral vision, her scales shimmered black. Twisting about she could glimpse a tail curving into two feathery moulded fins tipped with creamy gold. More surprising as she tasted the length of herself – her menses flow had stopped. Not stoppered up, or her insides twisted, it was simply *gone*.

"What about … both?" she suggested.

"Both." Grant nodded.

"Both is good." Izzy nodded back at Grant. "*Taniwha*."

"Tanny-wharr."

"You two finished?"

"Alright, alright. Hold your horses. Grant, turn around, I'm taking my shirt off."

"Izz, what does it matter he sees you? You're naked whenever you're a dog! And he's naked when he's a donkey! Come on!" The eelskin had sloughed away the well-trained barriers of her inhibition.

She itched to be off. Robbie's *need* pulled, and it grew fainter with every passing minute. Like something vital was passing out of him.

Grant blushed bright as sunburn. He left his pants on when he slipped into the water. His shoulders and ribs poked against his skin, bones too big for his flesh.

"What's happening?" His teeth chattered.

"I think if you hold on tight to these … tendril things, I'll be able to pull you through."

"To where?" Izzy sloshed into the water, still in her undergarments. The taste of her slid over Tea's eelskin and she fought to ignore such a delicious taunt. She was still human, deep down inside. None of this animal nonsense, not when she had a job to do!

"I'm not entirely sure. Africa, though I know it's a big continent. This water joins up to that water."

For the first time since the whole bally-hoo began, scepticism held Izzy taut. "That's a long way. Can you hold your breath that long?"

"Not something you need to ask me, I think." With barely a thought Tea elongated her feather-scale tail to match the undulation of the creek.

"I think … we can …" Grant closed his eyes, took a deep

breath, shook his head. "Come on, let's do this."

Tea tried to taste him like she could Izzy, but he was stronger in his reserved donkey ways.

How would these two land animal-people breathe? Though the journey must be thousands of miles, Tea knew it wouldn't take them thousands of miles of time to get there, but still enough time that dozens of breaths would be needed.

Sssswim ssssing.

The water wanted her to *sing* at them? Sing what? She only knew hymns and a few radio tunes by heart. And singing took breath away from breathing …

… but singing also expelled air.

Oh, dear lord. Tea's giggle burbled up.

"What's so funny?" Izzy glared into one of Tea's shining black-green eyes as she wrapped tendrils around both wrists. She shuddered at the rubbery texture.

"Don't worry, you won't hurt me, and they won't break off," Tea said. "And what's funny is how I figured out you're going to breathe underwater. I'll do it for you."

Grant's mouth went almost as round as Tea's. "Oh."

For some reason, Tea didn't care about kissing Grant. Izzy, on the other hand …

"Let's go," Tea burble-barked.

Grant found his grip on her tendrils and then as one they took deep breaths and dived under.

Yessssss.

Fists of water yanked them down, flinging them forward into a darkness spotted with pin pricks like stars. The fresh, cold-as-a-mountain limestone-tinted water became salted, heavy, abundant. The current pulled them along so fast she had no time to make sense of the creatures great and small, the scintillating layers, the depth and *age* of water. This water had passed through the cycle of the world countless times, touched everything. It held incredible knowledge. The enormous wealth filled and emptied Tea at the same time.

A tug on her right tendrils. Izzy, needing to breathe. Tea had been letting her own *air* just be. If she thought about it too hard – the slits in her neck, the slithering through her eel body – she might start choking. She took in a great *whisk-hum* of air and manipulated her tendrils. Izzy's face was right there.

No time to hesitate or think. She placed her mouth over Izzy's.

Not so much a kiss, but a sharing of life, of the water's song. A tingling along her edges. Somehow it felt far more intimate than anything romantic like the movies or books or magazines told.

She performed the ritual for Grant. Her edges did not tingle this time. She was getting used to the strange deal, she decided.

The current widened, narrowed, twisted, shoved them about. Tea slid along its imperative undertow easily, but she worried that the skin-bodies with death grips on her narrow whiskers were being battered. She brought them in closer, protecting them with her fins.

The ocean was not silent. Enormous shapes rushed by, moaning years-long songs. Beautiful and terrifying in their age, size, and complexity. Things deadly as knives, cutting through the water. Things tiny and clustered, life giving. The grating of metal on stone, sonorous and deep as a million years.

Water deliciously warm then urgently cold.

The *idea* of land rushed at her. They were flung through a narrow gap, then progress slowed enough for Tea to understand islands and peninsulas lurked like hooks ready to catch in her skin. A great mass anchoring the world to her right.

One more sharing of breath, and their headlong rush slowed to a more human understanding of time and space. The current threw them deep down one last time, a dry cold creaked around Tea's eelskin, and the wide-flung ocean became a pitch-black tunnel. Salt-sting turned mineral again, but this one lush as sun on clay, moisture biding its time between the cracks of heat and stone. Muffled noises leaked down, growing more wicked as Tea wriggled towards the surface.

As the three travellers popped up gasping for air, the noise stitched together into an abundance of pure evil. Shouts of terror, rage, and shooting stars.

No, not stars. Shells. Bullets. Bombs. Metal threads rattling the air.

"Oh my lord."

"Grant, are you alright?"

"I'm intact. Where are we?"

"I don't know. It's so dark. I need my canine nose. Tea?"

"Give me a moment." Tea let her scales thin towards flesh, peeling back her head to something more human. She was glad it was dark enough Grant and Izzy couldn't see. The air slapped her with a hundred things at once as she tasted it with eel and human senses. "Sunrise is hours off. We're in … an oasis, a few miles off the coast. I recognise the palms on the edge from my atlas. There are … buildings too, but they're empty. Sandbags. Barbed wire. Oh, God."

"What?" Izzy had unwrapped herself from Tea's tendrils and was paddling towards the edge.

"No. Don't!"

The stench hit Tea hard and strong. She'd got used to plucking chickens, mucky animals, and meat stripped in the cold store. But it hadn't prepared her for *this*. There was no direction she could swim to get away from it. It leaked into the water, staining its perfection.

Grant pushed alongside her, rubbing his arms, saying nothing.

"Now what?" Izzy's teeth chattered. For a desert place it was surprisingly cold. She'd been the toughest of the girls through frosty mornings, so it had to be more than the cold getting to her.

"Turn around, both of you, would you? I need to figure out how to change," Tea said. "The water … talks differently here."

"Righty ho," Izzy drawled, but they obliged.

"I forgot it would be spring here," Tea said, pulling at the water's song with her prickly senses. She'd become so used to the farm stream's song, she hadn't thought water in other parts of the world would have something different to say. "We need to find some clothes."

"For you, maybe. I plan to be running around in dog form. I don't know about you, Grant."

Grant mumbled something too low for Tea to hear.

Finally, Tea found the right tone in the water's song, an echo of home, a hum that told her it had passed through that place in its cycle an aeon ago. She pulled on the strand. It went taut and sang like a lone violin string but gave her enough to shift back to her human shape. Her joints snapped back into place with a pleasurable crick and pop and she once more had fingers and toes. She didn't dare pull too hard on the water's good temper; the hum turned to a screech in her temples as she attempted to flip her skin. She lost her scales but her skin remained dark. Strange, but good camouflage.

It would have to do under the circumstances, she decided.

With her flesh settled into more familiar lines, Tea's teeth took up a chattering she had no control over, and her heart pounded so hard her head throbbed. Without the armour of her full eelskin holding her together, old thoughts rushed back in: boys, marriage, war, death … Izzy. One upside to the mess: she remained eel enough that her menses stayed silent.

She rubbed her arms. "It's so cold. And loud. But quiet. Where is the fighting, exactly? Oh lord, Jerries could be all around us."

Izzy placed a hand on Tea's shoulder, but Tea flinched away. The comfort, Izzy's burn-bright skin, didn't feel right under the circumstances. "It's alright, Tea. Take a breath. Let's find you some clothes first."

Grant huddled in the sand as they rummaged through the rubble of houses and small barns. Bile surged in Tea's gullet at the sight of blackened bodies, human and animal.

Izzy found a dirty but serviceable robe that had once been pretty, with blue and white embroidery around the hem and neck. The linen wasn't thick, but the scent of the previous owner enveloped Tea in a cosy warmth she identified with hard work, sheep and smoke. She had a good feeling the owner had escaped, even if they'd had to leave most of their life behind to be trampled by the oncoming storm.

"Now what?"

Izzy sniffed the air, but it was Grant who answered.

"He's nearby."

"How do you know?"

With her vision made staccato by the flash of bomb shells, it was hard to read his face.

Grant rubbed his right hand, the sound like bone on paper. "I know."

"But I'm his sister. We're connected by blood, by whaiwhaiā."

"There are connections other than blood," Izzy murmured.

"Izz." Grant's eyes were too big and tired in his narrow face. "She'll know soon."

"Know what?"

Before Tea could question any more, the pain in her right arm flared into full flight, and she groaned. Izzy hissed her quiet.

"We don't know what side of the lines we're on. Which way do we go?"

Tea's arm jerked up, pain puppeteering her action, like someone had braided her muscles into a rope.

Grant pointed in the same direction at the same time.

South. Towards the greatest noise. Towards the shouting scent of charred iron.

Tea tried pulling on the water's song for relief, but it gave her little. Dredging up the practice she'd had at hiding her lady moments and the tears from Mum's slaps, she pushed her ragged nails into her other arm. The pain evened things out a little.

"I need to be less conspicuous." Grant's bones creaked as he took his mule shape too fast. Even his animal face held lines of sadness.

What did he have invested here? How could he feel Robbie so strongly?

As if hearing her thoughts, Izzy gripped her shoulder. "We're doing this together, alright?"

Tea bit her lip to stop a sob, and her chest tightened. *So this is what it is like to have true friends, not just people who tolerate having you nearby.*

Izzy nodded. Had she heard that, too? Was that part of her weird-wolfishness? Tea didn't like the idea of someone in her head without permission and Izzy nodded again, releasing her grip on her shoulder.

"Thank you," Tea whispered.

Her arm throbbed an imperative.

"Grant, you stay back," Izzy said, low and smooth. "Find an empty building to wait in. I know that doesn't sound too heroic, but I suspect we'll be needing your strong back. I'm going to scout in dog form. Tea, you—"

"I'm not hiding. My skin—" She flexed her hand. "—I can hide in the shadows with my skin like this."

"Sweet Mother of Jesus," the donkey muttered.

"*You* can talk." Tea didn't mean to snap, but the pain-strings were pulling her muscles and mind taut.

Was that a chuckle as Izzy shifted into her dog form, or the rustle of skin-fur?

"I can track you by scent," Izzy lisped from her dog mouth. "If you stop moving or find something, I'll be able to tell. If I find Robbie first, I'll come get you. Fair?"

"It will have to do." Tea sighed.

"Be careful." A big pink tongue scraped up Tea's cheek, then the border collie flung herself out past the palm trees.

"God damn, Izzy." Tea back handed the slobber off her cheek.

"Oh, sorry" She blushed a side-eye at Grant, who nodded his long head slowly.

"Take care."

Grant plodded off into the shadows behind a cluster of houses, his pace at odds with the fear and anger that gripped the darkness with talons too sharp.

Tea removed her robe and balled it up under one arm. Calling on the moisture embedded in the shadows to help trick the light around her, she found a dappling that would allow her to dodge from shadows to trees effectively.

After only a few steps, the enormity of the situation gripped her hard, and she had to steady herself against broken mud brick. She didn't know how to fight! She was just a girl from the bottom of the world in a land meant for no man at all. She was supposed to be marrying a good boy, not creeping around with her skin on display.

But the water song. On the tip of her tongue and her fingertips. *Yesss thiss iss your place your time.* It emanated off everything: rocks and sand, allowing Tea to taste and move smoothly amongst their shape and rise; the night sky punctured by the great exhalations from explosions and screams; the rustle of the nearby ocean and deep water table; the pizz-tang of metal; the sting of fear on skin.

Under different circumstances she could have spent forever exploring the whaiwhaiā of the place, all it could tell her about what was and what could be, but not in this now.

"Focus, Tea," she muttered, shaking her head to clear the disharmony of the night.

Further down the road giant vehicles with caterpillar treads ground along, their great arms reaching like angry monsters. Panzers, she remembered from the news reels. They belonged to the enemy. And the enemy looked like they held the line at a pass.

Between them and her, the ropes on her muscles pulled.

Give me something, please, she begged of the water song that didn't agree at all well with her southern senses.

The night parted, grudgingly. Movement amongst the dunes and trees, green as eel eyes.

There. A fling of ochre buildings, their sides caved in. A handful of troops huddled in what little cover the buildings and fallen palms could offer. Heads popping up from time to time, but bullets made them scurry. Others didn't move at all.

Tea pulled on the iron sting that rose like a clotted mist from the men. She could be hearing the water song all wrong. The blood of one man was no different to another, they could be Jerries.

But there; she couldn't mistake her brother. The pull she had only assumed as brotherly love, and now knew as their shared whaiwhaiā, was distressingly weak.

Tea crept as close as she dared, dragging the shadows with her.

What to do? She couldn't waltz up in her altogether. They would shoot her on the spot. And the borrowed robe, it could mark her as a foe. *Darn, botheration, and ... and ... shit!* She put her hand over her mouth to stop the terrible giggle from exploding out.

Tea bided a moment, rubbing dirt into the robe. If she was going to be caught, she decided, she wanted to do it clothed.

Come on, Izzy, she thought as hard as she could, wondering again if she had imagined her friend reading her mind before. *Where are you? Here I am. Help!*

She squinted, the corners of her eyes itching with a crust of sand and salt, and emanated her water song in all directions.

The fear-blood-salt-scent was upon her before she realised she'd let her focus drift too far away.

"What in the bloody blazes!"

Oh, sweet Jesus.

"What is it?"

"It's a girl. And she's a bloody darkie! You one of them Jerry whores? Don't you move, girlie, or you'll be breathing out new holes!"

8.

The water song off the gun aimed between Tea's eyes sizzled rotten. It trembled like a branch in a breeze.

"What you smiling about, girlie?" the soldier demanded. She couldn't see him well in the dark with his face all smudged with dirt and grease, but his accent was instantly recognisable as New Zealand. He rolled the Rs and rounded out the vowels. He was from deeper south, probably Gore way.

"N-n-nothing. I d-didn't … didn't realise I was, I was smiling." Her voice was barely a whisper.

"Well, bugger me."

"What you doing, Anderson?" came the other voice, closer now. "Who you got?"

"She looks like one of them local darkies, but she sounds like a Kiwi," Anderson mouthed off over his shoulder.

Still in a crouch, Tea's thighs took up a trembling ache. The battle raged on despite the conversation between gun and flesh.

The other man melted out of the shadows, blue eyes brittle within a crust of dirt. "Shut up, will ya. Gray's a darkie too. Geez, you're right. That is a girl."

"He is not," huffed Anderson. "Anyone can get a good tan in this godforsaken place."

"What you doing here, girl? All the locals were evacuated." Underneath the dirt the other man was all angles, blue eyes, and blond hair. Her type, according to Mum. Everyone had all made out the troops were too tough to be frightened, but the stench off this man – *No, he's barely stopped being a boy* – told her otherwise.

"I-I'm h-here to help, yes help." Tea swallowed. "You say Gray? Sapper Robbie Gray?"

All three ducked as a shell whizzed overhead, but Anderson went right back to staring her down, though the gun still wobbled.

"How the hell—?" His hard blue eyes dismissing her with one knife-cut glance, the blond turned to Anderson. "She's a spy. Shoot her."

"Wait!" Tea flinched as her voice caught on the cold air. "Robbie's my brother! I'm Tea! Dorothy Gray! Ask him!"

"All the way from New Zealand to visit her brother in a war zone," Blue Eyes sneered. "How sweet."

"It's true. I'm here to help. Please, take me to him, and I can prove it." Tea's whole body shook now, and her stomach went loose, like all her waters and the moon were about to rush out of her. How ignominious.

"She does look a bit like him, Trip," Anderson said, the gun wavering down an inch. "He said his sister was his twin. Maybe she's one of the girls, you know, from a forces club. Got worried. Came searching for him."

"All the way out here? The clubs are in Cairo, man!" Trip's jaw worked like he was chewing a tough piece of gristle. "How in the hells do you think *you* can help, girlie?"

Before Tea could muster a reply that might make sense, Anderson cursed at a flash in the dark. "Bugger me, there's a dog here."

Trip's eyes narrowed, and the water of his thoughts sent prickles down Tea's spine. "Must've got left behind."

"I think … I think I can get you to safety," Tea whispered.

Trip barked a low laugh. His terrible grin was picked out by the flashes of shells and starlight. He didn't even flinch at the delayed concussion from a bomb. "For all you know, we could be a forward advance team. Snipers. Pick them Jerries off, one by one. Pap pap pop!"

Tea flinched at the plosive words.

"Trip, the dog, for God's sake!" Andersons eyes were wide, like he was about to lose it laughing.

"Let me go to him," Tea plead.

Anderson gave her a quick one-handed pat down.

The most intimate a man has ever been with me, she thought. It meant nothing. She felt nothing, just his rough, shaking hand.

"Oh fer Chrissakes," Trip growled as Tea pushed into the maze of collapsed walls. Her thighs burned from crouching too long, and her water song thrummed high and cold with all the blood around her. So much blood.

"Robbie? Where are you?"

"Tea? What the …" Robbie's voiced wavered, whispery, like the water in it was draining out. Had he been away so long she'd forgotten the sound of him?

He huddled beneath a roof on a precarious lean. Izzy stood over another man in the corner, paws planted, fur vibrating with low growls. The man did nothing, just stared out from a mask of dirt, his eyes white against the dark. It took Tea a moment to realise the crust was all blood.

"Tea? It really is you!" Robbie wheezed. He reached out with his left hand, his right arm held tight against his chest like he was afraid something would fall out.

"This really is your sister?" Trip scoffed. "Well, now I've seen everything."

"And is that …"

"Yes, that's my dog, Izzy." Tea kneeled.

Trip took position behind her. Anderson had melted back into the darkness.

"How did you get here?" Robbie shivered violently though he was well dressed, his wool uniform mostly intact if incredibly dirty. His boots and gaiters were well broken in, the pants torn at the thigh, and the front of his vest weighed down by things in pockets she didn't want to examine. She only wanted to imagine Robbie butchering sheep, not other people.

"Not a story for now," she said. "Suffice to say it was a long journey."

"Christ, Trip, take a step backwards." Robbie's voice was a high-pitched whisper, but it still held authority.

Trip did so, but his hard stance held. "Are you out of your goddamn mind? We're fucking surrounded, probably dead, and you think your fucking sister from New-fucking-Zealand is here to save you?"

Tea flinched as the curses emulated bullets burying home in her flesh.

"We're … I'm here to help, and that's all that matters," Tea murmured, searching for what had incapacitated her brother.

The lines around his mouth and eyes looked like someone had taking a paring knife to his skin and scored in the borders of the countries he had crossed in the months he'd been away. This wasn't the brother she recognised. Though she did. He may have been the younger of the two of them before, but not anymore.

Robbie's right arm shook, though it didn't look damaged. His hand flickered in the low light, but the flesh was still human.

You're the stronger one, Grandad had whispered to her not long before he lost the ability to speak. Then she had thought he was being kind, but now? What had Grandad known he didn't think worthy of sharing?

Then she saw it. The tear in the hip of the pants went much deeper and darker, blood singing an ugly, dirty song. She was good at basic first aid – a scrape here, a cut from wire there – but she didn't know what she was looking at.

"What is this? What's going on here? What happened to you? Where exactly are we? Why didn't you help him? And why aren't you taking him to safety?"

Tea's voice rose higher on each demand. At the last, Trip's hand flinched as if readying to strike her, but he caught himself in time.

"How do you not know where we are? You're here, aren't you? And your brother? He's a bloody fool. Thought we could take out that one last bridge so the Panzers couldn't get across. Got too close. Stray bullet. We were corralled here." Trip ended up letting his hand flick in a dismissive gesture. "He's losing blood but when I went to touch him, he started shrieking like a girl. Had to stop first aid or he'd bring the Jerries right down on top of us."

"Took out the bridge, though. Boo-oom." Robbie laughed weakly. "Took some of them bastards with it. Worth it."

Tea didn't want to think about what was 'worth it'. She leaned in so her mouth was by her brother's ear. "Where are we?"

"Tunisia," Robbie whispered back, as if guessing she was here by no ordinary means. "Near Gabès. Past Tebaga Gap. The push was going … well."

Robbie put his head back against the wall and hugged his arm tighter. Tea had never heard of the place, but she had to guess it was real. This was all real, wasn't it?

"Fascinating," whisper-lisped another voice. "But that's not what we mean. How long have we got?"

"Izzy? That really you? Good God, how?" Robbie's eyes brightened for a moment.

Izzy had backed off from the man hunched in the corner, though her hackles remained raised. He stared at the three of them but made no comment about a talking dog. Tea hoped if he did, he put it down to shell shock. Whatever that was.

"Later." Izzy kept her voice low, muzzle near Robbie's face, as if licking him. "We have to get you out of here. All of you."

Tea brushed at the water song surrounding her brother, flinching at the piss-yellow red-clot taste-scent. It shouted, but didn't scream. The bullet wound might not kill him right away, but the poison slowly taking him over surely would.

"We thought we were getting around the edge of the Germans fine," Robbie said, voice cracking. "Then a Panzer came around and cut our retreat off. The rest of the British Eighth is somewhere back thataway." His free hand trembled towards the dark hump of dunes and blackened palms waving in the distance.

"May as well be all the way back home for all the hope we have of getting out of here."

Tea's giggle came out tinged with hysteria.

"I can't move, Izzy," Robbie whisper-groaned. "I want it to stop, but it won't. I held on as long as I could, but the bullet ... oh my God, it hurts, Izzy. It hurts."

Tea caught her friend in the snare of her glare. Why was her brother, the person she'd swum across the world for, asking Izzy for help? Had Izzy lied about not courting Robbie?

"What can't you stop coming?" Tea whispered furiously. What form did his whaiwhaiā take? Of course, he would be some strong animal. A stallion, maybe, or a lion. Perhaps a bear. Or moa, brought back from extinction?

"Izz, I'm sorry." The flickering from his hand manifested in his face. Flesh struggled against flesh.

"Shh, we're here to help," Izzy said. "How far to your battalion, do you think?"

"Half a mile, maybe. A bit more. But it doesn't matter. I can't walk. And it's coming, Izz. Any moment now. And the boys will see, and then ... I'll really be dead. Shot on sight. If not, court martial. Jail. Mental asylum."

"Do you think you could make it stop if Grant was here?"

"What are you on about?" Tea sunk her fingers into Izzy's ruff. Izzy snapped her teeth; just a warning.

"I swear to God, if Grant is here, I'll—"

"Tea, put pressure on that wound," Izzy ordered, voice disguised by a low growl. When Robbie shook his head, she added. "It's alright, Robbie. She's fire, too."

"Wha—"

"How you think we got here, you silly chook?" Tea grimaced. She tore off the hem of her robe and pressed it into the seeping wound. Robbie didn't even flinch at the pain. The flickering around his neck slowed.

"I'll be right back." Izzy melted into the gloaming, leaving behind her a warm scent that made Tea realise she was desperately hungry. It must be well past dinner time back home.

With his spare hand, Robbie positioned her in such a way that her body shielded him from the glare of the silent man in the corner. He hadn't moved in all this time, but his stillness spoke of a quick deadliness, a wrath Tea did not want to incur.

All at once, Robbie's face fell into repose. The pain and anguish didn't disappear, but the lines and angles changed in a subtle way. The L of his jaw softened, the folds of his eyes loosened, and his lips bruised up a little, like those nights he'd come home having been in a fight.

"Whaiwhaiā," he whispered.

He wasn't an animal. He was another person.

Tea glance-checked. Trip had turned his back and was conferring with Anderson. They both stared off into the dark, ignoring the man in the corner. "What ... *who* are you?"

"You're not surprised," Robbie said.

"I've seen too much in the last few months to be surprised by much, but this is getting up there." Tea smiled to soften her whispered words. "You can change. How ... how long?"

A stutter of bullets. Everyone flinched, except Corner Man.

"Since I was fifteen, before I went shearing," Robbie whispered, breathy, high-pitched from fright. "But the feeling, the tearing of it, has always been just below my skin."

She touch-checked his face, shoulder, hands – his tremor was a little less – and her brother smiled back. "You're not angry?"

In reply, Tea held up her hand. Pulling on the energy of blood, sweat, the cold air, she ran a ripple of scales down her flesh, webbed her fingers, lifted a soft fin up from her elbow. "Scared as heck, maybe. But not angry. You want to tell me what's going on with you?"

"N-not here. But I—" He winced at the pain, his own words. "I want to be, need to be … both people."

"Both who?" Fear warred with jealousy. Robbie had had so much more time to think about it all.

A chatter of voices. Tea didn't understand German, but the harsh, spitting syllables felt like a curved knife slashing the desert air. Everyone tensed, except the silent man. Tea held her breath until she started to see stars against the stars. Her heart beat so loud, she thought it alone would give them away.

After what seemed like a lifetime, the voices moved away. The shared pain in Tea's arm had spread into her chest, and she almost vomited spit when she breathed out.

"That was too close," Anderson growled, leaping from his crouch to stalk a straight line, back and forth, gun down, not coming too close. "We move now, or we don't move at all."

"Wait!" Tea plead, keeping herself between Robbie and them. "My friend will be back with help any moment!"

"This is a goddamn battlefield, girlie!" Trip growled. "There's no help coming! We're on our own. Oh my God. I'm arguing with a near-naked darkie girl. I'm dead already. I am. And this is hell. We're going, whether you're coming or not."

"A few minutes more, that's all we need, Tripplet." Robbie

coughed. "We haven't been spotted yet. That's an order."

"If a goddamn girlie and her dog can find us—"

"That's an *order*."

"Yessir." He snapped an insolent salute.

Tea cast about for Izzy's water song. Nothing. She was either too far away or very good at masking her scent.

The German voices were still in range. The near-sunrise air wafted their stink to her – crimson iron, grease, hot flesh. She grabbed Robbie's too-cold hands, suddenly too tired for words. The flickering translated into little sparks of lightning in her skin.

Hurry up, Izzy. Please.

A clop-chuff and pant-cough. A wet nose pushed into Tea's elbow, and the long sandy-grey head of a donkey swung around the broken wall.

Robbie gasped and flung his free arm around the donkey's neck. "I thought you were bloody joking when you said Grant was here."

Robbie clung to Grant as if his life depended on it. A whole new bunch of questions crowded into Tea's head.

No time for any of them.

"Great," Trip drawled. "Now there's a donkey. Will Noah row up with a boat to save us, too?"

"This donkey is going to get Robbie to safety," Tea snapped. Did he not want to survive this war? "It'll be a far sight faster than trying to walk him out. You coming?"

Trip threw up his hands. "Why not. It's all madness anyway."

Robbie muffled his groan as Tea helped him climb onto Grant's back. For a small, skinny man, Grant made a sturdy pack animal.

The sharp lines of Robbie's jaw and chest had returned. *That's some powerful touch Grant's got,* Tea marvelled. *More powerful than me.*

Fear, wonder, jealousy. A war within a war.

Robbie sat as dignified as he could, shaking and wounded atop a donkey. His bullet wound seeped at an alarming rate. "Brixt, take point as we head left around the dune."

The silent man didn't acknowledge the order, simply stood, took his gun, and disappeared around the side of the crumbled building.

Robbie sighed and looked over at what Tea had taken for a pile of rags. "We'll come back for you, lads."

Bodies. There had been bodies right by her. Tea's gorge rose, and she had to pull hard on the water song to keep her flesh intact and her voice inside her body.

As vulnerable as the bombed-out building had been, at least it had provided corners, shadows, shelter. Against the promise of day, Tea's composure shattered into something much more acute. Though it was dangerous to remove her attention from what little water she could touch in the ground, the blood soaking into the fine grains was too much to take. She needed all her energy to guide her brother and his friends to safety, not be concerned with her wretched retching.

At least the light was low. Spinning the water song into a shroud to encompass the other men made Tea's flesh and bones grind harder, so she had to trust the silent point man and his mask of bloody camouflage. Izzy stayed only a pace ahead of Grant. The sand shifted beneath their feet, but Grant held himself strong and sure.

"Did you hurt your arm at one point?" Tea whispered, disturbing Robbie from murmuring into Grant's woolly neck.

Robbie gave her an all-too-familiar expression: hard to read, calculating. "I thought I could control it without Grant around," he said. "But it got harder. Every time I had to … use my gun, my hand would shake, like something was trying to break out of me …"

Grant grunted as an explosion hit too close on the other side of a dune. He stopped in place, and the group hunched down for a moment. Tea lost herself by diving for the comfort of the water song in the ground. The water deep below emboldened her shroud, though it grated along her edges, unfamiliar with her touch.

A thump. Too light for an explosion, too round for a bullet. Another.

Tea's whaiwhaiā burned with the nearness of something salty and hot.

"Move, move," she whispered.

Trip turned a rude stare on her.

"Someone's coming." Her voice took on an urgency and authority she hadn't thought she could possess against a man. "Those trees beyond the dune. If we make them, we might be alright."

"That's some pretty fancy eyesight you got there, missy," Anderson whispered. His grim stare swiped a layer of filth over her perception.

The attack came swift, from above, a dark body flung down the dune.

A low shout covered by the rat-a-tat of bullets further off.

A thump of bodies. Grant froze; there was nowhere for him to go. Robbie reached for a gun, but his fingers shook so much he could not grasp it.

A dark uniform. Eyes glittering midnight blue below light hair. Fingers hooked.

Why didn't he shoot?

Fingers dug hard into Tea's shoulders.

Stars against stars, a bursting flurry of the Milky Way rotating about the Earth, about the war, thrusting their millennia of existence together in one impossible moment.

Stars. Against the black night of fur. Stars. A glint of fang. Stars. A burst of surprise, the white of the eye. Stars. An explosion of hot matter, a growl, a tear in the fabric of skin.

Dark stars, singing their ugly splatter across Tea's flesh.

Silence, as one patch of the world could be amongst the insanity of falling shells, bursting gunfire, and dying men.

The song, the scene, realigned itself into a reality that made sense but no sense at all. Izzy standing over the fallen man, four paws caging him, teeth bared, muzzle dark and wet, growling so low her canine-being vibrated nose to tail.

The man's – *the German's* – head was thrown back, throat exposed to the bone by a long gash. He did not move. Blood trickled weakly from the gaping wound, not the great pumping spurt that would suggest a heart in motion.

Tea retched.

"Jee-zus," whispered Anderson.

Trip glanced between the corpse and Izzy, face grim. "He must've been cut off, too. Probably caught him off guard." His voice shook only a little. "Let's go."

Izzy shook out her head and left the corpse sprawled in the sand.

Grant plodded forward, ever stalwart.

Tea didn't remember the steps between the body and the trees. A few bullets whizzed by, but not close enough to trouble Anderson and Trip unduly. Robbie kept his face buried in Grant's neck the whole time, whispering.

A challenge call. Tea almost flinched into taniwha shape – *No, Izzy, please don't do that again* – but the voice called to them in New Zealand-accented English.

They had made it. They'd found some of Robbie's Second Battalion mates.

"… local girl caught in the crossfire …"

"… got wounded, pinned down …"

"… helped us with her donkey …"

"… get her out of here quick …"

When Tea could make sense of things again, she was huddled inside a lean-to against a truck, a coat around her shoulders, a nurse looking in her eyes, testing her limbs.

"Not me, him." She gestured at Robbie huddled up against a now-kneeling Grant-donkey, already attended by a female nurse. *A woman, out here, near the front line? That was a thing that could happen?*

Her nurse finished his inspection anyway, frowning in confusion. He passed her a canteen, then left. Her tongue thick, her flesh creaking with overuse of the water song, Tea gratefully swallowed the tepid water. It stayed down, though it roiled in her stomach.

Izzy wriggled in beside her. "Tea, we have to go," she

whispered. "Some muckety-muck will be all over us in a moment, demanding answers."

"But Robbie. We can't leave him here."

"And we can't take him back with us. That would give everything away. And I doubt you have the energy to do it."

Tea sighed. "Wait. Please. I want to say goodbye."

Izzy growled low, an assent.

The nurse finished her triage of Robbie leg. He struggled over with Grant's assistance. Tea leapt up to hug her brother, afraid to let him go. Izzy twined between their legs, shivering agitation.

"Thank you for coming for me," Robbie murmured. Pain etched his face into puzzle pieces Tea might not be able to put together again, but at least those edges were softer. "I wouldn't have made it without you or Izz. Without Grant."

Grant squeezed behind the truck pulled hard up against a stand of rock. A pop of bones, then he sighed. Making a barricade with her body again, Tea peered around the hood taller than her head. In the pre-dawn light Grant's flesh was very pale, his eyes jaundiced.

Holding Izzy's ruff and Tea's shoulder, Robbie tottered into the narrow space.

Then he took Grant in his arms and kissed him.

Kissed him!

That was *illegal!*

A flicker passed over Robbie, head to feet. For a moment, his hair lengthened into tatty but proud victory rolls. Shoulders narrowed, chest broadened, hips curved out, beard disappeared, cheekbones became taut, lips plumped up, and eyelashes lengthened.

Oh. *Oh. Like me, but unlike me.*

Tea stared, eyes so wide she felt them drying up in the cold air.

Robbie's other self, his whaiwhaiā, was a *herself*. A beautiful self.

"What ... how—"

"Later," Izzy whispered, nudging at her shins. "Grant. Change. *Now.*"

Thankfully no-one was nearby when Tea peered back around the truck. She slid out and beckoned to the others that the coast was clear.

She helped Robbie slide into a seated position in the lean-to. "I've got to go. I'm sorry. I wish I could stay and help more—"

"You've done more than enough." Robbie grasped her right arm, hard, and the old constant friend of pain slid away to a murmur. "I—I'm proud of you."

Her brother. *Sister?* Proud of her. The idea pounded through her head, circling round the image of her brother kissing another man.

Tea could find no words other than a useless goodbye. With a clench of her fist, she pulled the shroud of shadows around them. As the ground sang the tell-tale song of approaching footsteps, they slipped farther into the stand of rocks.

Tea took one last look back. Her heart almost squeezed its way out through her ribs. The strange silent soldier, Brixt, stood sentry at the end of the truck, his gaze on their retreat as if he could see through the shadows Tea made dance to her song.

Then the crust of blood cracked around his thin mouth. He nodded and raised his hand in farewell.

9.

"Oh gosh, I've stolen some soldier's jacket."

"Under the circumstances, it's the least of your worries. Hey, aren't we going the wrong way?"

"We can't go back the way we came, Izz. I smell water this way. Um, is that a well cover?"

"Huh. So it is. Grant, you all right there?"

"Tired."

"Hang on. We're almost home. So, what does water smell like?"

"It's different everywhere. This one ... ow, these steps are steep, sorry Grant. This one smells the way cold off tin tastes."

"Right-oh. Oh. Well, you're getting quicker at it."

"That one hurt. Everything hurts. Come on, hurry up. I want to get out of ... this place. Grant?"

"I'm ready. Izz?"

"Your scales really are very pretty."

"Izzy!"

"Nah nah, don't fash yourself. Let me get out ... of ... this ..."

"Ohhhh. That didn't sound good."

"Hush. I'm hungry."

*

"Where in all the bloody hells have you three been!"

"Sorry, Mr MacGregor. The pig went bush. Took us ages to track."

The farmer grunted. "Why the hell are all three of you wet?"

"The pig charged Tea and we fell in the river getting out of its way."

"Well, that was bloody stupid of you. Hmph. Sure you weren't up to no shenanigans up there? Better be no bloody shenanigans. I'll have your guts for garters, ladies. You'd be out of here in a moment!"

"No, sir. I absolutely swear, sir. I would never do wrong by the girls."

"Hmmh. There's nothing to be smirking about here, Miss Gray. You didn't even bring the bloody pig back!"

"Not grinning, sir. Just cold."

"Mind your lip. Well? What are you waiting for? Get the horses unhitched and get back up to the bloody house! Your dinner's getting cold. And I'm sure Mrs MacGregor will have a word or two for you."

"Yessir."

"And don't think you're finished with that pig either. First job after milking tomorrow is get back out there and shoot that sunuvabitch. I don't want it scaring up my ewes."

"Yessir."

*

"There you are."

"Izzy! How many times have I told you? Don't sneak up on me like that."

"Sorry. Habit. Gosh, I could almost see your tonsils there."

"Sorry. I'm bushwhacked. It's been, uh, a long day. Ha."

"It's all right. Alison and Carmel are still up at the farmhouse with their knitting. And seems you're not so tired that you have your skin sitting right."

"Thanks. Oh, silly … there I go … yawning again. Mmh. The water sings right, now we're home. Where's Grant? Is he all right?"

"Out like a light. Sleeping like the dead."

"Don't say that."

"Sorry."

"No, I … I mean. Is he … what happened … back there …"

"You're not upset? Going to the police?"

"The police? No! That's my brother! They're friends. And their whaiwhaiā … mixes. And … oh, I don't know. I'm very tired, and it all feels like a bit of a bad dream."

"Bad?"

"No … no, I mean … yes, it's bad. Illegal bad. I can't stop thinking that. But the way they … Robbie looked like, like life had been put back into him when they … when they …"

"Kissed. I know. It's hard to say it. Was for me the first time I found out about it."

"It. Mmh. Oh, apologies for my noisy tummy. I don't know why, but I'm still hungry, even after that extra potato and slice of mutton."

"You didn't get pudding—"

"—that was a shame."

"—but I have something to make up for it. Tah dah!"

"Are those Soldier Crispies?"

"Is that what you townies call them? Yes, Anzac biscuits."

"Izzy, where did get them?"

"Didn't steal them from Mrs MacGregor's fête stash if that's what you're thinking. No, she gave them to me. Said they were to make up for missing out on the steamed pudding."

"Oh, thank you. Mmm, delicious. But … that's not like Mrs MacGregor at all!"

"She's not all 'Get to doing those dishes, girls!' and watching you with binoculars from the veranda. Besides, she said it was a waste chucking the pudding out to the dogs. Not that she was being altruistic, of course."

"Of course."

"She also sent me back with this."

"What is it?"

"Don't know. She said not to open it until I got to the cottage. C'mon, scooch over. Thanks. Biscuit? Ta. What … oh. Oh, my giddy aunt."

"What are they?"

"You've never seen them before? They're French Letters."

"But they don't look like letters, or French. Let me read the label. It's spelled dee you are … Izz, are you all right? Don't choke on your biscuit."

"Uh-huh. Oh gosh. Um. How to explain this. Tea. They're … prophylactics. Because, we might be up to, er, shenanigans?"

"Prophy … oh my gosh! Izzy! Put them away! Why on earth would Mrs MacGregor think we needed *those*?! It's not like there's anyone here ... stop it! Stop laughing! It's not funny! Get out of here and take those ... things with you!"

"Shenanigans!"

"Hey! If you're going, leave the biscuits!"

10.

Tea cradled the unloaded rifle as she stared up the paddocks.

This was as close as she would get to looking like a real soldier in the war. There would be no telling anyone what they had done, and that made it feel like the ground was pulling her body down.

The search for the wild pig over for the day, she carefully packed the gun away in its case and saddlebag. The beast was proving wilier than anticipated, or so they had explained to Mr MacGregor after fruitless hunts. They satisfied his humour by returning each time with extra possum fur, which got good money in town. But wild pork would make a nice change to the dinner table, so they kept going out whenever they had free time. Tea could *taste* the pigs out there. And it was a good excuse to be alone with Izzy and Grant.

The familiar landscape wasn't quiet as a normal person would imagine. No matter how dry the wind, it pushed water drops around in the air. The creek murmured nearby, the river that fed it large and unforgiving. Far beneath her feet, masses of water moved through the earth; the soil alive, underground rivers forever refreshing the cycle of water.

There were fences, trees, hedges and sheds between her and the farmhouse, but with the grip of water she could taste the position of animals, and where each of the farm workers were. Mr MacGregor was settled in for the night with his papers and letters, the other girls were in the cottage, Grant in the barn, and Izzy ...

"You have the fire going already. Thanks." Izzy threw down three possum corpses, shooing off the eager dogs.

"Kindling was damp. I found a way to make it ... not damp." Tea tried not to look at the possums. She didn't know why the dead pests would make her uncomfortable. She'd seen worse.

"You're getting better at it each day." Izzy crouched to rinse her hands in the creak.

"I felt you coming this time." Tea checked the billy. The tea was looking nice and dark. "Only by about a minute, but that's better than usual. I lose you when you disappear too far into your dogskin."

"You're welcome. Been practising. I keep forgetting that I can relax a little. Now there's there three of us. Not too much though. Thanks for having my back."

"You're welcome yourself."

Tea twitched her shoulders, avoiding Izzy's gaze. The last few nights, just before sinking into exhausted rest, she had been thinking far too much of that exchange of breath they had shared during the rescue. "Grant coming?"

"Later. Tending to the horses." Izzy whumped to the ground by the fire with a big doggy sigh and began stripping down her gun.

Tea fiddled with a stick, singeing the end in the flames.

"Talking to them, you mean. He's been doing that more since … since we came back."

"He says it keeps him in touch with the earth."

Izzy shot her a curious look. "It keeps him grounded—"

"Funny ha ha."

"—you know what I mean. He worries about Robbie all the time. And he's not allowed to show it. It burns him up."

"Sorry. I'm still getting used to the idea of … well, you know." Tea sniffed the air. Now it was dark, Grant had relaxed into his donkey form and was with the horses in the lower field, shielded by hedges.

The tired lines of Izzy's face softened as she bobbed her head to catch Tea's eyes. Tea couldn't help but smile at her friend's persistent warmth. "You sound more worried about them being together than Robbie's other skin."

"I know. It doesn't make sense to me either. Why didn't you tell me about them and his whaiwhaiā letting him be a girl when he wants to?"

Rifle dismantled and packed, Izzy dug around in a saddlebag. "Wasn't my place. Us animal changers, whatever we are. We have to hide who we are, or we'd be in terrible danger. Somehow, we find each other. Maybe that's the whaiwhaiā, blood talking to blood. But the silence, the caution? Those are rules which have held the three of us together for years. Now the four of us. It's no-one's place to speak for someone else. If we did, we wouldn't be able to trust the other again."

"In a way, I'm glad Robbie has someone to take care of him, because he used to get in so many fights." Tea paid careful attention to winding damper dough onto a stick. "Oh! I think

I understand that bit now! But I'm still mad at him. For not trusting me."

"You should tell Robbie *and* Grant that. Among other things." Izzy's rummaging produced a flask and two tin mugs.

"I ... I'll try." Tea carefully balanced the damper above the flames. "I received a letter from Mum, by the way. She told me about the telegram from Robbie's battalion. About him being injured in combat."

Izzy grasped her chest dramatically. "Oh, what a terrible surprise," she said, flat toned, smirking.

"Izzy. Be respectful."

"Sorry. Go on."

"He was taken back to London to recuperate. Something about complications. He'll be on one of the hospital ships in a few months, maybe stopping over in Fiji for R and R. He'll be home before Christmas." Tea said the last with a long shaky letting-out of breath.

"That's wonderful news! Does Grant know?"

Tea nodded emphatically; he had been the first she showed the letter to.

"Good. Do you think Robbie will be put on desk duty?"

"I don't know. He can't abide sitting still for long. I doubt they'll discharge him so he can return to the farm. There's ... still a lot to do in this war."

"That there is," Izzy sighed. "But it's good news, at least. Grant will be pleased to have him home. At least, within these shores."

"We all will."

With the cheerful fire crackling, dogs and horses drowsing,

and the cicadas singing, Tea had nothing to do, nowhere to look. She twisted her empty hands together.

Izzy raised the sloshing flask. "That deserves a celebration."

"Izzy what have you done?" Her friend held the open flask out for her to sniff, and Tea recoiled in horror. "Beer?"

"Mm-hmm."

"But this is a dry district! Mr MacGregor would fire you on the spot if he found you with it!"

"Oh, stop with the naïve act." Izzy raised an eyebrow, adding another interesting angle to her face. "You don't have to keep up the chaste bit around me. Come on, girl. Relax."

Heat rose up Tea's neck that had nothing to do with the fire. Some old habits were hard to break, but Izzy was right. Working here on the farm, with her friends, was polishing off her hard edges.

"How did you get it?"

"Why do you think the milk cans coming back off the evening train from Dunners are just as heavy as when we sent them in the morning?" Izzy chuckled.

"Clever!"

"There's always ways around the prohibition. Don't tell anyone. Go on. Try some."

"I don't know … "

"You've had sherry before."

"Yes, but … "

"Alright. Hmmm. What does its water song say?"

Tea inched her nose closer to the flask mouth again and took a deep breath. "Tobacco. Bread. Smoke. Fire. Night sky. Oh. Oh! Intriguing. Ah, g'awn Izz. Give me a sip then." Izzy splashed a mouthful of the amber liquid into a cup, and it made a pleasant froth that tickled Tea's nose. She giggled, rubbing the tip. "Mmmm. Well. I … don't hate it. Alright. Pour me a cup."

"Don't drink too fast, or your head will get all woolly. The damper will take a while to bake." The planes of Izzy's face changed again, a little strange softness chipping away at the cunning and tiredness. "Turn it, eh. It's too crispy underneath."

They sat in silence for a while, watching the fire sending embers up into the sky. Tea sank into the quiet, the air between them filled with the complex water from their bodies and breath. Again, Tea found herself wondering what Tea's breath tasted like up close in her human skin. She took a big gulp of beer and it fizzled warm in her chest.

"So, what happens now?" she asked, not sure what to do with the silence now she had loaded it like a cloud full of rain.

"What do you mean?"

Izzy looked directly at her, and Tea shivered a little. She grasped her cup, determined to hold that gaze a little longer.

"You and me and Grant. Here, the farm. The war."

"We … I think we carry on."

"With what? How? Why?"

"The war isn't over. That means the Land Service isn't over. We still have jobs as long as they need us."

"I hope it … I want it to last longer than that. Forever maybe. Not the war, I mean. But this."

"Dorothy Gray, are you telling me you're shedding your townie skin?" Izzy smirked over the rim of her cup.

Hold on, keep looking a little longer, Tea told herself. It got easier with each passing moment.

"I can't help it. I like it out here. It's quiet. And I'm doing something useful." She ran a rough hand over her chin, nose, and cheeks, scratching her skin gently. *Skin above skin.* "But I want the war to be over, too. The water, the air, the fighting, the blood—" Tea let out a long breath. "It pulls me every which way. Hurting. In different ways to what I feel through my connection to Robbie and to ... to this place."

"Oh, Tea." Izzy didn't reach out a hand in comfort, and Tea was grateful for that. She didn't know how she would cope with the touch of Izzy's fingers on top of everything else filling her head and skin.

"But there's also something fresh and clean in the air. Very far away, but ... there. Do you smell it too? Please tell me you do. How the water song stretches on beyond what is here *now*. That there's *something* ahead. Though I can't *reach* it. It tells me there's something more for us, though I can't imagine how, with Robbie and Grant. You. And me. Gosh, me working a *real* job like this."

"I smell it. And we'll work it out. Work through it. Towards that fresh air. Together." Izzy raised her hand from her lap, clenched her fingers as if she were trying to decide something, and let it drop again.

"Oh, Izz. I need to forget it." Tea shook her head and held out her cup for a refill. "I need to think about a real future, finding a husband, like Mum says I should. Once all the boys come back they'll want their jobs back, and then what will I do?"

"How often has your mother been right? Or even truthful about where you come from?"

"Izzy! That's my *mother* you're talking about!"

"I know. And you are not her." Izzy punctuated her words with a pointed finger, a very manly thing to do. In other company, it would be shocking. In Izzy's company … it just made her more *Izzy*. "You're more like Robbie. You have a strength you have to get comfortable with. Make friends with it. It makes us different, girls like us. But we wouldn't have it any other way."

Needing the cool comfort of water, Tea unfolded from beside the fire and strode towards the creek, beer in hand. Izzy was right, it was making her head a little woolly. But it was made from water. She could figure out a way to make it stop, perhaps.

But she didn't want to. The mix of cool and warm, the smoothing of her edges, felt nice.

Izzy followed discreetly, giving her just enough space, but still too close. "Why, Dorothy Gray. Are you blushing?"

Tea put a palm to her face. "Isabel Larson! You stop grinning right this instant."

"Why? I'm *proud* of you. By God, woman. You were incredible. That eel thing you became. The taniwha. You were a dark, luminous being. A spirit of the water."

"You've been reading far too much poetry."

"And you don't read enough." Izzy's voice dropped a little, as cool-warm as the water Tea sought solace from.

"It's not something we ever had in the house."

Another cool-warm touch. Skin against skin. Izzy's fingers questioning against Tea's free hand. Tea's knuckles went white around her cup.

"Izzy, stop that. Girls don't hold hands." Tea didn't pull away though.

"They should. Friends need to look after each other. Comfort each other in dark times like this." Izzy watched the play of the silver dark against the creek. "Hey, slow down with the beer. If it really is your first time drinking, you don't want to get sick on it."

Friends. Comfort.

"Thank you." Tea put her cup down on a rock, Izzy holding her steady by the hand. *Holding her* ... "You, saying you're proud of me. You were there too. You were so *strong*. You held it together, held your form, when I couldn't. I was so afraid. I'm sorry if I let you down."

"You didn't let me down. Why would you think that? We all did what we were good at."

"Are you ... good at ... God, I can't remember it straight." Tea shuddered and Izzy squeezed her fingers gently. "What you did to that Jerry."

"I acted in the moment. I didn't think." Izzy's voice came as if from very far away, a little lost on the wind until the breeze wound around them, safe again. "It was either the Jerry or us. Sometimes I go further into being a dog than I should."

The eels – *my friends* – playing just under the surface of the shining, inky water gave Tea the courage to say the right words. "I'll be here to bring you back."

Silence again. Them, the water, the sky.

"Are you alright with this?" Izzy squeezed her hand again.

"I ... don't know." Tea bit her lip, trying, *trying*, to look Izzy in the face. "It's what boys do at dances. When they want your attention, to possess you away from the other boys." She gasped. "Does this mean you ... you're really a boy inside? Like Robbie, except the other way around?"

Izzy chuckled, the sound as warm as her skin. "I'm a girl. If a bit of a filthy one from the farmyard. Who smells like dogs. And one who … who is unsure of exactly what she is, but doing the best she can in a strange world."

"Izz?" It was Tea's turn to squeeze fingers. *Gentle now. How much is too much?*

Izzy shrugged. "You say you didn't know your dad. I don't get on so well with my parents. I guess they have their own things going on. They—I think they might be a little afraid of my whai-whaiā. No, not afraid *of* it. Afraid for me."

Tea chewed over all this for a moment as she watched the eels. Mr MacGregor never said anything about Izzy's Māori-ness, like he'd decided just not to *see* it. But he still said horrible things about Māori people. She hadn't realised how hard that must be for her friend. She couldn't do anything to stop Mr MacGregor without jeopardising their jobs, but she could be kinder to Izzy about it, try to understand. And just like being – *say it, say it!* – a homosexual was illegal, a white person being friends with, *liking*, a Māori was treated with disdain.

Were the whispers about her mother true? Tea let this digest, too. And she realised … she was scared, but *it didn't matter.*

"You—" Tea swallowed against the tightness in her throat, the threatening tears. "You're beautiful. And strong. I know you're not supposed to say that about girls. But I *like* that about you. There are lots of different things about all of us sitting under our skin. We're all connected. What was it you said? We'd work it all out together."

"I thought you said you didn't read poetry." Izzy cleared her throat with a swallow of beer, and chuckled. "Did you mean it when you said I was beautiful?"

"Well, neither of us will win prizes at the A and P show. But … to me you are. And I … like dogs. They're comfortable, and furry. And loyal." Tea's hand trembled only a little as she took back Izzy's hand, which felt gentle and firm at the same time.

"Hey now." Izzy stepped closer, putting her cup next to Tea's. "What's this?"

"Just letting you know that we're … friends."

"How many boys have you kissed, Dorothy Gray?"

"Umm?" Tea could look at Izzy's chin now. And her lips. "Two. But they don't really count. They weren't nice at all. I guess that's what being with boys is. They're rough and awful."

"Did Robbie and Grant together look rough and awful to you?"

"N-no?"

"Tea, you're trembling."

"It's cold."

"Here, let me warm you up."

Tea managed to meet Izzy's eyes just as she came in to press her lips against hers. She lost her vision for a moment. It was everything and far more than she had imagined, her dreams like monsters, but ones that could stop the war, *the world*, with their power. If they, *she*, tried hard enough.

"You taste like beer." Izzy's lips smiled against Tea's.

"Izz … oh. What was that?"

"What it's … meant to be? Was it alright that I did it? I can stop if you want." Izzy touched her cheek. *There* it was again. That fizz Tea felt when they exchanged breath, breathed together, in the water.

"No, it's ..." Tea murmured, biting her lip, looking up through her lashes. "I don't know."

"Auē. It's not wrong, Tea." Izzy cupped her cheek, skin raw and soft and warm all at the same time, full of all the things she could do. "We're not wrong. Like Robbie and Grant aren't wrong. Like our whaiwhaiā isn't wrong. Listen, what does your water song tell you?"

Tea mirrored Izzy's gesture, touching her cheek. "That ... I need to try again. And listen harder. I don't know if I got it right the first time."

The eels danced against each other.

EPILOGUE

Tea sat at the farm office desk, cold cup of tea at her elbow, willing the phone to ring. She could taste the intent, the buzz along the line, as well as she could taste the electricity in the sky before a storm.

The sizzle came from two directions, both north. It was almost four, so Robin would be calling from wherever she and Grant were in their Auckland celebratory escapades. The second sizzle of intention came from around Wellington: it had to be Benny.

Noise filled the farmhouse – barking and the friendly shouts of the kids and work gang from the yard, the wireless in the living room, and a cat whining impatiently for attention at the bay window – but Tea's focus landed on the office noticeboard. The usual planting and work gang schedules and reminders of doctors' appointments were covered by newspaper clippings from around the country. The one pinned on top had just arrived in the mail from a friend in Christchurch. Front page of *The Press*, July 10, 1986. 'Five votes pass homosexual law reform'. Was it only just over a week ago? A victory still fresh and keen as VE and VJ day, though the battles were forty years apart.

Tea poked the old memories like a broken tooth: the girls in their uniforms, whistled and jeered at by the crowds. But for the land girls, there had been no medals, no commendation from Parliament. Just silence. Tea and Izzy had kept their uniforms out of spite, and the home office had stopped asking after a while.

Their uniforms now were the same as they had been for decades – gumboots, dungarees, and mud – but it felt lighter somehow. She'd walked out into each freezing dawn for the last week with her shoulders straighter, her head held higher. It didn't matter anymore if some nosy neighbour riding past saw her and Izzy leave the old farmhouse together, or saw Robbie and Grant exit the other house on the property.

Maybe.

A battalion of women had ended up making the land theirs despite the discomfort of a changing world. The other farmers in the area either tolerated or welcomed the two 'married' couples who had bought out the MacGregor farm after the old couple became too infirm to manage the large property. A couple of local families even embraced them. Unmarried aunties and uncles who 'lived together' were good referees for them at The Office, their nickname for the Ministry of Social Welfare.

The Gray-Stevenson farm had become a home for kids just as lost as the four of them had been. The gay kids, kids with whai-whaiā, kids who wanted to change like Uncle Robbie into Aunty Robin, but for forever.

The law reform battle had been won, but another was brewing. Searching for the warmth she knew was hibernating in the winter ground, she pushed her thoughts down into the earth, her whaiwhaiā threading around the soil clumps like her winding eels dancing through the water. Something tasted off, tasted *ill*. The something Benny had gone looking for, her whaiwhaiā pulling her away from her foster home on the farm into a nursing career.

The whistle of the kettle on the Shacklock and the rattle of cups startled Tea back into the breathing world. She flicked away the scales darkening her fingertips with the old irritation, and her hands became her hands again, bent by a little arthritis and scarred and dried by a lot of time.

Izzy swung into the office with a tray of cups and biscuits.

"She's late calling," Izzy grumbled, then muttered something in te reo. Tea let her buzz-cut voice settle into her, the constant harmony to her water song. "I told you Grant shouldn't have gone to Auckland so soon after that bad bout of bronchitis."

"The girls are probably still having a whale of a party." Tea gratefully took a fresh cup and dunked a gingernut. Though both houses had been renovated to electricity early, there was something about tea brewed on the old wood stove, or from the billy. "And Grant knows how to look after himself."

"Pft. You always make excuses for them." Izzy grimaced at the wall as if she could still see the ugly roses of the MacGregors' old master bedroom they'd painted over years ago.

"I do not! They worked so hard for, God, *years* to help change the law." If Izzy saw ugly roses in the office, Tea saw Grant patiently typing submission after submission, making phone calls and newsletters. "They deserve to celebrate. Robin needs to be in her skin for a while."

"We worked hard, too," Izzy grunted, easing into the old

green velvet chair in the corner. "People forget that so quick."

"Robin and Grant don't."

It had taken some convincing from Izzy, but they'd joined the Lesbian Coalition to help with the campaign. Not because Tea didn't want to help, but she was endlessly cautious. One misstep and they could lose everything they'd built with the farm. They were both excited by the watershed moment, but they couldn't help but feel the sting of how the official language centred men. Their friends in the Auckland and Sydney clubs – the girls, their old foster kids – were miffed. "Even with all the organising work we did, they just want us dykes and trannies to stop existing," Tina had drawled in her cigarette-and-whiskey voice down the phone as disco thumped in the background.

Tea hated when Tina spoke that way, but deep down she knew she was right. Robin was still getting into fights even in her sixties. Benny had gotten into scuffles at nursing school, too.

Izzy stared at the ceiling, muttered in te reo again, then blew out a breath. "Sorry. I'm just so—"

"Tired. I know."

"The air is tight." Izzy squeezed a fist, the wrinkles on her face making a map Tea couldn't read for a moment. But then after a moment gazing at her love – hair grey as a storm, but her shoulders still muscular and lean – there it was. The old warmth building up – simmering coals, summer winds, sweat from hard work, the belly heat from beer – that had held them together for so long.

"You feel it, too," Tea said. "The water song doesn't taste right. As if it's stagnant from sitting too long."

Izzy locked gazes with Tea. "Is it like … before?"

"No. But it's something big, getting bigger, a new battle. Like when Robbie and Grant went to New York in '69. Like when you marched on Parliament in '77. I think Benny is about to call."

Izzy's gaze strayed towards the news clipping. "It's that virus."

The phone shrilled. They flinched.

"Aunty," Benny sobbed down the line. "I need your help. People are trying, they are, that little girl's story made a difference. But there are so many. I can't make it stop. I don't know where to take them or what to do." Blood and piss and death were in her voice, fear like black scabs, tighter than the loose yellow of cancer that had taken Tea's mother back in '58.

Tea fell into practised soothing of Benny's stone armour; stone that had gotten her into so much trouble, stone Tea had learned to carve with the gentle trickle of water. Izzy grabbed the long-wired extension and murmured in the warm tones she used when Benny had awoken from her nightmares as a teen.

When Benny was coherent enough, she told them about the people left alone to die in America, even by the hospitals. The water song grew loud and tight in Tea's head. Her skin itched, scales creaking and flickering up to her wrists. An old call to arms.

A solution tumbled from Tea's lips as easy-hard as changing into her eelskin had come all those decades ago. "Let's bring some of them here, eh? There's plenty of room in both houses. You're not alone. We'll fight this together."

Tea rubbed the fingers of her right hand together; that old pain was mostly a whisper now. Without having to hear their voice, Tea knew her sibling agreed. Grant too; whatever the kids needed, he was there with pride.

Pride. A word she heard more often these days. Izzy's back straightened and she nodded firmly. "Ae, together," she said.

ACKNOWLEDGEMENTS

This book has its origin story in a second-hand bookshop. The cover of Dianne Bardsley's *The Land Girls: In a Man's World, 1939–1946* (University of Otago Press, 2000) – a muscular, tanned woman shearing a sheep – leapt out at me and planted the double-meaning story title in my head. Bardsley's patient research on this part of forgotten New Zealand women's history was an indispensable resource, and helped me formulate the characters.

Thanks to Fiona in the Tūranga archives for helping me research homosexual law reform. To books on the women's military auxiliaries and war work force by Bee Dawson (*Spreading Their Wings: New Zealand WAAF in Wartime*, Penguin, 2004), Bathia MacKenzie (*The WAAF Book*, Whitcoulls Publishers, 1982), and Deborah Montgomerie (*The Women's War: New Zealand Women 1939–1945*, Auckland University Press, 2001). And to the National Library online photograph collections which helped with images of the uniform and land girls at work.

Thanks to my family who supplied memories of the Dunedin to Palmerston train services and North Otago during wartime, to my great uncle's wartime letters, and my grandfather's war service in the Middle East.

This book wouldn't have happened without the enthusiasm of editor and publisher Marie Hodgkinson. Thanks to Laya Rose for the beautiful cover art. Kia ora Cassie Hart for the sensitivity read.

Thanks to my critique group CLAM who helped with my original drafts, to beta reader Andi C. Buchanan, and the rest of the Crustaceans for your support.

I wouldn't be the author I am today without my Clarion classmates and tutors. It's an honour to have you as colleagues and friends. Special thanks to Ann VanderMeer for her advice and unwavering support.

And love and thanks to C for always being there.

ABOUT THE AUTHOR

A.J. Fitzwater lives between the cracks of Christchurch, New Zealand. The Clarions Writer's Workshop of 2014 presented them to the world somewhat formed, and two Sir Julius Vogel Awards are used interchangeably on any given day as unicorn horns. Their short fiction can be found in a variety of anthologies and such venues of repute as *Fireside Fiction*, *Clarkesworld*, *Beneath Ceaseless Skies*, *Shimmer Magazine*, *GigaNotoSaurus*, and *GlitterShip*.

ALSO FROM PAPER ROAD PRESS

THE STONE WĒTĀ
OCTAVIA CADE

We talk about the tyranny of distance a lot in this country. That distance will not save us.

When the cold war of data preservation turns bloody – and then explosive – an underground network of scientists, all working in isolation, must decide how much they are willing to risk for the truth. For themselves, their colleagues, and their future.

Murder on Antarctic ice. A university lecturer's car, found abandoned on a desert road. And the first crewed mission to colonise Mars, isolated and vulnerable in the depths of space.

How far would you go to save the world?

FROM A SHADOW GRAVE
ANDI C. BUCHANAN

Wellington, 1931. Seventeen-year-old Phyllis Symons's body is discovered in the Mount Victoria tunnel construction site.

Eighty years later, Aroha Brooke is determined to save her life.

"Haunting in every sense of the word"
– Charles Payseur, Quick Sip Reviews

AT THE EDGE
EDITED BY DAN RABARTS AND LEE MURRAY

From the brink of civilisation, the fringe of reason, and the border of reality, come 22 stories infused with the bloody-minded spirit of the Antipodes.

Winner of the Sir Julius Vogel Award for Best Collected Work, 2017

"Lovecraftian horrors to please the most cosmic of palates" – Angela Slatter

SHORTCUTS: TRACK 1
EDITED BY MARIE HODGKINSON

Strange tales of Aotearoa New Zealand. Seven Kiwi authors weave stories of people and creatures displaced in time and space, risky odysseys, and dangerous discoveries.

Winner of the Sir Julius Vogel Award for Best Novella: Octavia Cade, *The Ghost of Matter*

"Six of the best" – Phillip Mann

BABY TEETH: BITE-SIZED TALES OF TERROR
EDITED BY DAN RABARTS AND LEE MURRAY

Kids say the creepiest things. Twenty-seven stories about the strange, unexpected, and downright terrifying sides of parenthood.

Leave the lights on tonight. So you'll see them coming.

Winner of the Sir Julius Vogel Award for Best Collected Work, 2014

Winner of the Australian Shadows Award for Edited Publication, 2014

CPSIA information can be obtained
at www.ICGtesting.com
Printed in the USA
LVHW030449150721
692684LV00007B/916